The Song They Sang

The Song They Sang

Brendan O'Byrne

**TWO HEADS
PUBLISHING**

The Author

Brendan O'Byrne was born in Dublin in 1912. His previous books include *Wilsons Place*, the story of his Dublin childhood, and *Ocean Queen*, on his career as a Naval Officer.

His short stories have been read on BBC radio and published in newspapers from Ireland to New Zealand. Still active as a writer, he is in his eighties and enjoys retirement in the tranquillity of the Cotswolds.

Acknowledgements

The author would like to express his
thanks to Esther Whitby for recognising
that this novel deserved to be published.

Thanks to Catherine O'Rourke of
Wexford County Library for her expert
help in locating and selecting the image
which appears on the cover of this book.

The cover photograph is of the memorial
in Enniscorthy erected to commemorate
the 1798 rebellion. It was originally
published in the early part of this
century by Mr Valentine and is
part of a collection held by
The National Library
in Dublin.

First published in 1994 by

**Two Heads
Publishing**
12A Franklyn Suite
The Priory
Haywards Heath
West Sussex
RH16 3LB

Copyright © Brendan O'Byrne 1994

A catalogue record for this book is available from the
British Library.

ISBN   1-897850-35-2

Cover Design by Kalligraphic Design, Horley, Surrey

Printed & bound by Caldra House Ltd., Hove, Sussex

ONE

'Now thank we all our God with heart and hand and voices'.

The Reverend Barnaby Scrase-Greene, Rector of Saint Luke's in the village of Gorteen which lies in a gentle fold of the Wicklow hills, led the singing with a will. The words issued strangely from the narrow mouth in the jowly face and his portly body seemed to swell with satisfaction as he praised his Lord in a mellow baritone so fervently that he threatened to drown the efforts of little Miss Etchingham on the harmonium. For once again had victory been given to the right and that same victory over the forces of evil would be celebrated in churches great and small all over the far-flung empire on this most joyful of days.

There was much to be grateful for. The greatest war in the history of mankind had passed Gorteen with nothing worse than rumours and the imagined echoes of distant guns although it was known that in Rathnew, hard by Wicklow town and known as the 'khaki village', hardly a house was not in mourning for a father or a son or both.

It was true that young Andrew Aylmer from the big house of Ardnagoilte had been killed on the first day of the battle of the Somme and that a couple of village lads had also been lost, but taking it by and large life had gone on in Gorteen much as always had. Except for things like tea and sugar country dwellers had no reason to experience the shortages of mainland Britain. And he had no difficulty making his usual monthly trip to the Kildare Street Club in Dublin to meet old friends from college days to swap opinions on the latest news from the front, for Dublin reckoned to know everything about the war before it became known in London.

The Rector's face, ruddy from pate to chin from healthy outdoor living, beamed as he reflected again on the invincibility of the England from which his forebears had come in Elizabethan times and if he felt himself superior to the mere Irish of the other church then he had reason and more for it. As he so often said at the Club, both races had been on earth for the same period of time. One had prospered by diligence and hard work while the other had remained in the same rut for hundreds of years because it lacked the will to climb out of it. It was an unanswerable argument, not that anyone known to the Reverend Barnaby Scrase-Greene would have been inclined to dispute it. The Irish were lazy, indolent and superstitious, of that there could be no doubt. One only had to look at them. The native Irish, that is.

Now he thanked his familiar God that his own only child, Captain Simon Scrase-Greene had come through the war safely and with honour. In his sermon (text Psalm 65; O Lord Thou hast dealt graciously with Thy servant) he would be proud to inform the congregation that Simon had been granted the inestimable privilege of entering the sacred city as a humble pilgrim on foot behind that great Christian gentleman General Allenby and that he would undoubtedly be visiting his old home at Gorteen as soon as the army released him, though the Rector privately thought Simon would probably go first to Newry to see Margaret and the children. A delicious piece of news best kept to himself for the moment was that the Bishop, an old friend of Trinity days, had tacitly hinted that Simon might have the living of Rosgarman, only ten miles away, if he so wished which would bring the family happily together again.

At the thought his eye sought to catch the eye of his own dearly beloved wife Flavia, seated at the far end of the third row from the front. In the Church or Ireland wives of clerics below the dignity of Canon are expected to know and to keep their proper place, to manage somehow to be both prominent in church affairs and self-effacing at the same time.

Again the Rector thought of God's great goodness to him and his and blessed the day thirty years back when through the good offices of Flavia's kinsman Lord Glenore he had obtained preferment and come to spend his life in this pleasant place where the strife and troubles of city livings were unknown. It had been as near perfect as anywhere on earth may be and he was well content. May God be praised!

Flavia Scrase-Greene, grey haired and bulky as her husband and looking oddly similar to him in features and colouring, knew that he was looking towards her for theirs was that sort of marriage, a union soberly entered into because it was suitable but which over the years moulded them to be one in mind and habit.

She knew too that he would also be thinking of the gangling lad who had surprisingly grown to be a man with a Simon of his own, and a Barnaby and a Roger. Conscious that she should not be asking favours of the Deity as the Catholics did, as if the great God himself could be persuaded by vulgar bargaining, her own secret prayer was that Simon and Margaret would contrive between them to give her a grand-daughter. For there was not a lot of pleasure to be found in boys and she did so want a little girl to make a fuss of as she had wanted one of her own all her married life. About the only thing she did not uncritically admire in her husband was his indifference to what in the privacy of her own mind she called the physical side of marriage. When Simon had been noisily ushered into the world in a nursing home on Mount Street Barnaby seemed to think he had done all that could reasonably be expected of him and proceeded to expend his considerable energies on the hunting field or crossing the hill to cast for trout in the Avonmore if he was not engrossed in things which happened in Greece thousands of years ago. Not that he neglected his parochial duties in any way: with a congregation of at most thirty souls there were few duties to be neglected and about the only times he ever raised his voice in her hearing was when some one had written to the 'Irish Times' about Home Rule, as if such a thing would ever be allowed to happen.

A shaft of wintry sunlight crept across Knocknagowna and struck coldly through the rose window above the unadorned altar to cast a fleeting glory on all assembled in the austere little church. As if directed to the purpose if seemed to illuminate the stark beauty of the young widow, Constance Aylmer, shadowing the high cheekbones and striking little flashes of light from the mass of red-gold hair beneath the ugly black hat which was the badge of her widowhood.

Silently she mouthed the word of the hymn, thinking in a kind of panic that no longer would she be able to hide her own tragedy in the greater tragedy of the war. For soon it would be all over and forgotten while she would have to go on living with that empty sense of loss for something she did not quite understand, missing something she had never had and trying very hard not to blame poor Andrew for it. It would have been much better if they had not married at all but it seemed to have been expected of them. And when Andrew presented himself at the Deasy home in Roscommon in the uniform of a captain in the Leinsters it seemed to be the decent thing to do. For the war was going badly in France and she could hardly have refused a man who might have volunteered to go to his death. As indeed he had, and that within a matter of weeks.

Maybe because of the euphoria of war the actual wedding had been rather nice and quite exciting. By the influence of uncle Middleton another uncle, James the Bishop had sealed their union in the chapel of Dublin Castle and the reception had been the big event of the Dublin season that year. Saint Patrick's Hall had been thronged with the very best of Irish society and some had risked the dangerous sea crossing from England. Cousin Erskine had brought his dear little American wife over for the occasion and a very stolid man he had grown to be, laconic in conversation and brooding a lot. They said that writers were often like that even if there appeared to be little of the successful writer in the slight man dressed in the uniform of a Lieutenant Commander of the Royal Naval Air Service who spoke only when he was required to and then only in the tersest terms. But his manners had been impeccable and when he smiled he looked really handsome.

The walls of the little church seemed to be closing in on her as she wondered how she could possibly get through the rest of her life without going mad. For Deasy women were notoriously long-lived and at twenty-four years of age as much as half a century loomed bleakly ahead, maybe even more than that, and how could she possibly fill in that much time confined by widowhood to the house and grounds of Ardnagoilte; for that was what it amounted to. It would be at least a year before she could go hunting again and as far as any sort of social life was concerned - dinners, balls, race parties, that sort of thing - everyone would be too considerate to expect her to share the pleasant rituals of their class. Being the widow of a war hero with nothing else to do but be kind to dear Lavinia who was not to blame for being a cripple, although there were some who thought that a tiny woman like her should never have put her horse at a six-foot wall just to keep ahead of the field.

Poor Lavinia! With the best will in the world she could not help being a burden and it would be a mercy if she just went quietly in her sleep one night for she would never get over the death of Andrew. But maybe Rory would be bringing a bride back with him from France or wherever it was the Dublins had got to when the guns were finally silenced, some suitable person to whom she could hand over Ardnagoilte and its responsibilities gracefully. Anyone would do. Any race. Any religion. Just as long as she could bow herself off the stage without unpleasantness.

A child would have helped although two would have been better for without children marriage was rather a pointless exercise. Maybe if it had not been wartime, if they had managed to get to London or Paris, the honeymoon would not have been the unmitigated fiasco that it was. She could still see the heavy old furniture and smell the salt damp of the bedroom of that miserable railway hotel on the West Coast with the Atlantic roaring its abuse the whole night and poor dear Andrew apologetically blaming himself for not being able, as he called it, 'come up to scratch'. Maid like she had relied upon Andrew to steer her through the initiation but it turned out that he also was a virgin, which surprised her very much because she had always imagined that men by their very nature were prepared for marriage well in advance.

So she still did not know what all the fuss was about, all the poems and the operas, the sagas and the legends, although she dearly wished to. For the messy charade in the big damp bed at Mulranny had kindled a need in her which became more urgent with every desolate night that passed, troubling her body and confusing her mind until she could think of nothing else. And now it seemed that need would never be satisfied.

Lavinia, the Honourable Mrs Lavinia Beresford-Aylmer ignored the pain in her back and sat rigidly on the special chair they always placed in the aisle for her since the day a badly judged 'leap' had robbed her of the use of her legs. Her small, fine-featured head of sparse white hair was held proudly erect. The rheumy eyes which gave away no secrets looked straight ahead, her mouth was tightly closed and the trembling of her palsied hands was hidden in the rug across her knees. If her heart was not already broken it would surely break now in the hollowness of this bitter thanksgiving.

Let the other praise their God for ending the war. She would always blame Him for allowing it to begin and for not taking more care of poor Andrew, the firstborn and most loved son whom she would mourn as long as breath was left in her. There was too much Aylmer in Rory for her to feel anything more than affection for him. He was a nice enough boy and very well liked but that, she thought, as much as could be said for her second son. Rory was an Aylmer but Andrew had been true Beresford of Waterford and it was Andrew she mourned unceasingly night and day. Now she blamed that uncaring God for taking the wrong son from her. If He had to have sacrifices why should it always be the finest and best loved? Why not take Rory in his place or that boy of Scrase-Green's or half a dozen other boys from the village? Although they hardly counted in the reckoning, Papists and Fenians every last one of them.

Her face set and stern she was acutely conscious of Constance sitting next to her at the end of the family pew. And she resented her daughter-in-law, for her pain had to be vented somewhere and surely it must have been Constance's fault that Andrew went off to war when he had no need to with Ardnagoilte and

14

two hundred acres of the best land in Ireland to care for. It would have been to please <u>her</u> that he went to find his death in the mudfilled trenches of the Somme. Lavinia would never forgive her for that though she would never show her bitterness openly. For old people develop a certain animal cunning, they have to if they are to survive in a world of which they are heartily sick but fear to leave it case the next world proves to be infinitely worse.

Once she had dreamed September dreams of seeing Andrew a man much like his father maturing into age with sons at his side, and if that dream had been granted she would have been willing to take her place in the little cemetery just inside the boundary wall of the demense. Constance had not figured in that dream. In the dream Andrew had wedded himself to a fine, strapping girl like Florence Goodwin from Rangyle, a girl who was knowledgeable about horses and cattle; able to run house and estate alike with a firm and uncompromising hand, a woman with enough sense to command her servants instead of acting as if she had no rights in the place at all. But with all her faults Constance tried to be a good daughter-in-law. Certainly she was better than any of the stupid girls they called servants nowadays and she would be there to read the papers to her and make china tea the way she liked it when the Mollys and the Marys and the Bridgets had all taken themselves off to spawn more of their own kind at the behest of some uncouth farmhand.

And there was a certain justice in the arrangement. Constance it was who took Andrew from her. So Constance would have the pay the price. The Deasys, she thought scornfully, who on earth had ever heard of the Deasys outside Roscommon? But everyone knew the Beresfords of Waterford and she would be glad when all this nonsense was over and done with so that she could get back to the big chair before the fire in the long, low drawing-room or Ardnagoilte. Really, one would think that a man of Scrase-Green's age would have enough sense to know that all this hymn-singing only got on peoples' nerves.

The brownfaced little man with the grizzled head was Vice-Admiral Reginald Barry and he did not really hold with all this religious stuff. But one had to set an example, which was why he had come over from Iveraun in his best go-ashore uniform of black and gold to join his compatriots in celebrating the victory of the old country over the heinous Bôche and to show the natives once again who was, very properly, the boss hereabouts.

The few decorations on his left breast were purely pacific which was a great sorrow to him. It had just happened that his naval service coincided with a period of unwanted peace with little more to do than show the flag in places like Trincomallee and the China station and the only shots he had ever heard were directed against a floating target. Which was not a hell of a lot to talk about when younger men could tell tales of Jutland and the Dover Patrol as if they were no more than ordinary experiences. Not for the first time he thought that without a war to fight a man might as well have gone into trade as far as honour was concerned. But that would never have done either.

His eighty years lay lightly upon him as he bellowed the words of the hymn. To him singing meant making as much noise as possible though what gratification the man above might get from all this caterwauling he could not imagine. But it was a ritual of the tribe -the Ascendancy tribe - and he would die before he denied his heritage. And he was proud of his country for, apart from that shabby business in 1916, Ireland had played her part well. On land and sea and now in the air Irishmen had manned the ship of state through the treacherous currents of war until it came safely back to harbour again and it would be many a long day before any blasted German - or anyone else for the matter of that - dared trail his coat to that England of which Ireland was indubitably and inseparably a part. He would have been very proud to hear his own son's name read out in the Roll of Honour. But bachelors do not have sons. As least none that they can own to. So that privilege was also denied him.

The people around him were not putting enough fervour into

16

their singing as if this was just another Sunday to be endured and as a duty to show the flag to the aliens beyond the pale. Needed geeing-up, that was it. Summoning all his reserves he bellowed so loudly that several people had to change key and poor Miss Etchingham pedalled the harmonium as if by that means she could escape the fury of the frustrated admiral.

At the back of the church beyond the tacitly agreed boundary of the baptismal font, in sober churchgoing clothes with gloves and prayers books, were the house servants, which means not those who worked in the house but those allowed to sleep in the house.

Catholics, it was generally agreed, were all right in their own way but it was wisest to keep to one's own persuasion and there was an element of duty in it. In place of honour on the aisle was Mrs Comiskey, the cook, as longnosed a Presbyterian as ever signed the Covenant. Alongside and in descending order of importance were fiftyish Mr Scoiles, the houseman, forty-year old Maggie Watkins, nominally the parlourmaid but whose duties took her into every nook and cranny in the house, Nellie Walker who assisted both Maggie Watkins and Mr Scoiles and a weedy looking lad who had been taken in as a matter of charity from an orphanage in Dublin.

Elsewhere in the church Nolan the cowman and his brood praised the Lord in unison with old Paddy Clery who did not rightly know what religion he was and Jeremiah Booker a staunch Methodist and the only man in the village who had any understanding of the workings of the internal combustion engine. The only Methodist in Gorteen Jeremiah was without any proper place of worship of his own and though he did not hold with the ways of the established church he attended this service to demonstrate before all men his unswerving loyalty to His Majesty King George the Fifth and because Catholic car owners were very few and far between in Wicklow.

The Rector raised his right hand to pronounce the Blessing and immediately Miss Etchingham spread her fingers and struck a great chord from the harmonium as the deeply loved

17

tune of 'God Save The King' swelled and filled the little church with all the nostalgic fervour of exiledom. For these people were exiles of several hundred years whose hearts were still anchored in a land beyond the Irish Sea where all things were good and vileness unknown. At the last verse the Rector slipped out through the sacristy door to greet his congregation as they left the church.

Again strict precedence had to be observed, which meant that no one could move before the people from the big house. And they could not move until Mrs Beresford-Aylmer had been helped to her feet and carefully escorted to where her dog carriage waited in the care of one of the village boys who had simply been bidden to the duty. As he waited the Rector sniffed the dewsweet air and fancied he caught a whiff of tomcat, which meant there was a fox nearby, maybe in the churchyard itself among the mossed headstones, and he thought 'We'll have that lad out in the morning' as he turned to offer his hand and his thanks to the patroness of his living. When all had gone their several ways he too headed for home and lunch in the ivied Rectory a few yards up the lane from the church, feeling beyond all doubting that God was truly in His heaven and that all would be well with the world evermore.

TWO

Saint Luke's, built by and for the convenience of the big house, lay camouflaged under an ancient tangle of ivy on the edge of the village as if anxious not to draw attention to itself. The 'other church', the Catholic church of Saint Laurence O'Toole in Gorteen proper was a much larger building, newer and more assured of its right to dominate the village and all who dwelt therein. Wide steps led up to the great doorway with beside them the grotto of Our Lady of Lourdes with a halo of electric bulbs and a French peasant girl kneeling in adoration before it. From a stunted rose bush scapulars and scraps of bandage hung as testimonials to cures obtained by praying at this shrine. It was not the church which designated this as a place deserving of veneration but the people themselves, looking to the stone statue with its fading blues and golds, who placed all their trust in some visible object much as their ancestors had in ages long past: for the very poor survive and live on hope alone. The church in its infinite wisdom simply allowed them to do so.

'Introibo ad altare Dei'.

The old priest Father Gilligan bowed low at the foot of the three steps representing the tortuous ascent of Calvary at the commencement of ten o'clock Mass, last Mass of the day, and took his time before straightening his body again. For the years were telling on him and what kept him going was mostly a fear of the sort of place they sent priests to when they could no longer discharge their parochial duties, comfortable enough places but with too many priests for his liking and not enough children.

Thirty years had Peter Gilligan been Parish Priest of Gorteen and the mere thought of being exiled from it brought a chill to his heart, for this village was more surely his home than the home of his childhood in distant Connemara. The congregation behind him shuffling as they tried to make themselves comfortable on the wooden kneelers or told their beads in

19

sibilant whispers were all individually known to him. Most of them he had baptised and many of them he had married. Not a few of them had he comforted in the hour of their greatest trial. So well did he know each and every one of them that he only had to look at a face to recall instantly a boy or a girl wearing the white rosette of First Communion or the red rosette of Confirmation. For all of them he had a strong affection which he did not know was love, which he imagined to be quite something else and outside his own experience. The thought that he might one day have to leave them troubled him even now, and what right had a priest of God to indulge himself in emotions which he had forsworn the day he entered Maynooth.

The sacred vestments were a burden on his frail shoulders as he laboured upwards to where the tabernacle was hidden by curtains of gold brocade, the words of the ritual spilling from his mouth unnoticed in the habit of almost a lifetime. At the first of the Consecration bells he sank on one knee and gripped the edge of the altar as a spasm of pain short through him and he wondered how it was that the doctors had not yet found a cure for a simple complaint like piles which plagued priests and wondering if they also got them in the Church of Ireland. If they did not would not be through too much praying for it was precious little prayin' them fellas did with their huntin' and shootin' and their motor cars and all their orders. A right oul' mess O'Reilly had made of the sermon, quoting scripture to people who thought the Bible a Protestant book. Little stories was what they liked. Unless it was a missioner, a Marist Father maybe, to frighten them out of their lives with hellfire and damnation. They liked that.

The Book had been passed back from the epistle side to the gospel side of the altar and he imagined he could smell his breakfast eggs frying in the Presbytery next door. That they were frying already he had no doubt for that woman never thought an egg was properly fried until it had turned black. Mostly they were like that. Priests' housekeepers, that is. About the only time in his life he had tasted a decently cooked egg was that place in Euston the time they went on pilgrimage to

Lourdes. And the tea would be stewed as well.

The Catholic church knows itself to be a religion of sinners and is very tolerant of human frailty. So it is that the obligation to hear Mass has through time come to mean simply to attend at Mass, to be within the church while Mass is being said to avoid the stigma and punishment due to sin.

So it was when Dermot Keogh shouldered his way into the packed porch of Saint Laurence's, indifferent to the protests of like-minded men whose one thought was to get out of the church in case Oul' Gilligan detained them for five minutes longer by inflicting a Benediction on them. Dipping his forefinger in the holy water font he sketched the sign of the cross briefly and muttered the Our Father, the Hail Mary and the Glory Be in one long and unpunctuated sentence although his heart and his thoughts were still far away over the hills in Dublin.

For things were happening in Dublin that Gorteen would never guess of. In Gorteen Easter Week 1916 was over and done with a few more names added to Ireland's doleful roll of Martyrs. Again the fight had been fought and again it had been lost and little anyone in Gorteen had cared because it was not by fighting the English that men kept their families clothed and fed. And what good had it done anyway?

Some good had it done. It had caused the hand of Destiny to rest on the shoulder of a giant of a man from County Cork who had actually been out in the rebellion and been interned in Frongoch in consequence. Incarcerated where the wind blew icily off Bala he considered his countrymen with an analytical eye. They were, the big man decided, great wavers of flags and singers of patriotic ballads but they jibbed when it came to the test. In 1916 the muster roll of the Irish Volunteers had a strength of 30,000 men but when the call to rebellion had come not even a tithe of that number had answered. So this strangely practical Irishman who dreamed great dreams for his country started to recruit selectively for his own army of hard men each to be separately shaped to be a weapon in his own hands.

Every man in Frongoch was qualified b his very presence there but not all of them were suited to his purpose. Some had only emotionally been committed to the cause of Irish freedom. Some felt their duty had already been done. Others were sullenly resentful of the bumptious young man from some godforsaken place in Cork who now presumed leadership over men who had been old in the movement when he had been pen pushing in a London post office, which in itself made his loyalty at least questionable.

Such men Collins held in respect but not in awe as he went about his business among what must have been the greatest concentration of rebellious Irishry that could have been devised, probing and picking his men and preaching the faith that the battle continued, that rebellion had not ended in the courtyard of Kilmainham Jail, that faith would be kept with the dead. But there would be no more glorious sacrifices. Henceforth the enemy would be attacked by stealth and with the least possible risk. For England was rich and powerful and accustomed to winning while poor little Ireland expected defeat, because that was the way it had always been. For quantity Collins wanted quality, fewer men closely organised and directed by commanders of inflexible will who would do his bidding exactly and without question, such an army of patriots as Ireland had never assembled in all its history before.

This it was Dermot Keogh had heard in a Stoneybatter pub when he had driven his beasts through the dampsweet night alive with sounds never heard by day and along the cowpatted North Circular Road to the cattle market and to refresh himself in a smoke-grimed public house where for the first time he heard the glorious news that Ireland was not accepting subjection to the vile English crown yet. At the news the blood ran shouting through his veins, for it was a great sorrow to him that he had not been 'out in Sixteen' although he would have been only fourteen year old at the time. Vinny Byrne of Dublin was just rising twelve when he found himself facing men hardened by battle in France and Jimmy Doyle of Carnew was not more than sixteen when he and six others held 800 of the Sherwood Foresters at Mount Street Bridge and killed or wounded a quarter of them. And Gorteen had done nothing.

As the Mass ended the men about him surged towards the door and his mind was made up. This very day he would cross the hill to Carnew, seek out Jimmy Doyle and beg admission to Michael Collins' Irish Republican Army. And if he was to end on the gallows for it, then so be it.

The smoke-blackened pot of green cabbage was being reduced to a tasteless mush as the Widow Mangan singed the pig's cheek for the Sunday dinner. As the bristles recoiled from the red-hot poker, flared briefly and charred with an acrid pungency the tinny bell of Saint Laurence's rang six times to mark the solemn moment of Consecration. The widow bobbed her head and murmured 'Lord, I am not worthy that Thou should enter under my roof' while yet resenting the poverty which kept her from Mass for want of a decent coat to her back.

In the good days before Joe Mangan had been found dead on a pile of stones with his chipping hammer still in his right hand going to Mass had been the big event of her week, the sanctity and the mystery of Good made flesh and the pleasant chatting with neighbours outside Byrne's public house before they all dispersed homewards with the blessing of God within them.

Those had indeed been the good days with Joe bringing home a pound regular each week so they never wanted for anything. But after he was taken it looked like the poorhouse for the lot of them until old Mrs Aylmer stepped in and said they need pay no more rent (for like the rest of Gorteen they lived on Aylmer land). And why should they? she asked herself indignantly, for what was only a bit of a tigeen at the back of beyond that hadn't been thatched since oul' God's time so that on sunny days you could see right through it and even the rats had left, most of them anyway. But for a Prodestan the oul' wan had been as good a Christian as she knew how. Larry could go across the field for milk any time they liked and every October a big farm cart dumped a load of cut logs outside the door so they could have a fire throughout the winter when the wind swept viciously over Knocknagowna and night began in the afternoon.

But that thatch niggled her. Surely the oul' melt could see the way of it every time she passed in that contraption of hers she called a dog-cart? And if herself did not offer to send the man to put it right then Lizzie Mangan would not be the one to beg her. For she still had her pride and if she could only afford it she'd soon tell the oul' witch what she could do with her milk and her logs so she would. But poor people cannot afford to show their pride and the half-crown they paid her every week for doing the washing of the big house, the sheets and the pillowslips, the towels and the tablecloths and all the bits and pieces, everything but their own personal washing - and that was done by that ugly Maggie Watkins that'd do anything to keep in with the gentry - made all the difference with six children to rear and ne'er a wan've them earning yet. And like as not when she collected her money the oul' man would tell her to go to the kitchen to see if cook had anything for her and sometimes it would be something good like the short end of a ham or shinbone with plenty of meat left on it - if the oul' bitch hadn't already given it to one of the Prodestans. Times Lizzie had a mind to take her offering back to the lady to see if the cook had been doing her out: but there is a certain propriety about even the meanest of gifts and anyway one Prodestan would never go against another; so she forced herself to be humble and went away nursing her grievance like a precious possession.

She dropped the grinning cheek into the boiling water and threw in a handful of salt. As if she could actually hear the priest intoning the valediction 'Ite Missa est' she crossed herself and started to load the biggest pot with scoured potatoes.

To the sight she was a little woman cascading shapelessly in bulging folds from her neck to her stomach, strong dark hair silver veined and her face roughened and reddened by the winds which sliced across the hillside the whole year through. Her sloe-like eyes were eternally watchful and she wore what she would have called her 'oul' pinny', a garment of unvarying

24

design with holes for her neck and her thick, muscular arms. Even at second sight she looked to be half as old again as her forty years and in her secret heart she recognised only the old gods of the river and the oak grove, and even from them she did not expect much.

In the pungent steam rising from the cooking pots she saw the sentimental vision of life as it should have been if only God paid attention to his business and spared a little for the needy instead of heaping more on those who already had enough of the world's goods. Then a tumult erupted through the doorway and she lashed out at whichever head happened to be nearest. The children had arrived home from Mass. In self defence Larry grabbed the big enamel jug and set off across the field to the dairy while swarthy Eileen piled the knives and forks in the centre of the deal table.

THREE

When Rory Aylmer came jogging up the rutted drive in Jerry Shanahan's van his mother's first thought was that perhaps she should have given his old clothes to the widow Mangan's lad. For two years in the army had broadened her younger son and for one breathtaking moment it seemed that maybe her prayers had been answered and it was Andrew come home again to take his rightful place as master of Ardnagoilte.

This was a Rory she had never seen before. In place of the openfaced boy who went laughing off to war was a man with a disconcerting wariness in his eyes and an assuredness which made him seem to be almost a stranger. She stifled the selfish thought of how happy she would be if it was her eldest son climbing off the ramshackle van and the younger in an unmarked grave somewhere in France. Instantly she regretted the thought. They were both her sons and much as she had loved Andrew, Rory was also of her flesh and blood, the new master of Ardnagoilte and landlord of all the eye could see from the ivied portico where she now waited to bid him welcome home.

They had never been an emotional family and the few conventional sentences and the light kiss on her cheek were all she expected in the way of affection. And if there was a strange reserve in his manner that too was an Aylmer characteristic and not to be wondered at in a man who had seen war at its worst in faraway France.

But it was at dinner that night that she realised how very much her son had changed and how utterly different he now was to any Aylmer she had ever known. To honour Rory's return the company had included the Scrase-Greenes and the Laceys from Rathcorney with their very suitable daughter Jessica who was of an age with Rory to bear him company. Constance, grimly bright and looking like a Lavery painting in her widow's black, was also present and the Admiral had ridden over from Iveraun to pay his respects and had, of course, been asked to stay to dinner.

It had not been a very easy meal. Constance looked ready to burst into tears every time she looked at Rory sitting in her husband's place at the head of the table. Through sheer nervousness Jessica made herself seem to be more of a fool than she actually was and the Admiral would go on and on about the China station as if they had all not heard it too many times before. No one seemed at ease and Lavinia was a good enough hostess to blame herself for that.

A week later would have been time enough for this dinner but she somehow had not relished the thought of herself, dear Constance and Rory dining alone without other company. Perhaps she could have handled it differently, quite how she could not readily imagine for there was not much in the way of company in this part of Wicklow, none that could be invited informally anyway.

At least the wine had been good, as it should be considering it cost four-and-six the bottle, and Rory had had his glass refilled at least five times with the port and brandy still to come, so she hoped he had developed a head for liquor and would not disgrace them all at table. There was something faintly ominous in the way he propped his arms on the table so that Walker could not clear his plate to allow the pudding to be served, and his eyes glittered wickedly. Andrew used to look like that in drink but poor dear Andrew never did anything worse than somersault along the corridor or jump over the balustrade into the rose garden.

There had never been any real harm in Andrew but of Rory she was less sure. It occurred to her that she really knew very little about her youngest son and it would be a fault in her that she had always preferred his brother. But then Andrew had always been there while no one was ever very sure where Rory might be at any given time. And he was such a secretive boy, leaving the house and returning without ever saying where he had been or who with and at times it seemed he was on better terms with the servants than with his own family. She wished the Admiral would cease monopolising the conversation, such as it was. Everyone was sick and tired hearing about the rebellion as if it had happened only yesterday. She coughed to attract her son's attention and inclined her head towards his plate.

He looked up startled to realise that he had been holding up the meal. Then he leaned back to allow the flustered maidservant to remove his plate while Maggie Watkins became very busy ladling gooseberry fool from the Sèvres bowl which no one was allowed to wash but herself into little silver timbales each of which she decorated with a small macaroon biscuit. As Maggie started to fan out extra biscuits Rory gave Nellie what his mother thought of as a too friendly smile and said, as to an equal 'Sorry, Nellie. Tell cook that was very good', which was not quite the done thing especially as Lavinia intended to have a word with cook in the morning about the mutton being underdone and the absence of caper sauce. Setting her mouth severely she waited while the girls served and cleared off. When the meal was finally ended and she was sure they were not hanging about outside the green baize door listening to every word being said she would have to do something to stop the Admiral whether he liked it or not. But one could not be too careful where staff were concerned. One indiscreet word could be misinterpreted and relayed all over the barony in no time at all. Staff, she told herself for at least the thousandth time, had to be kept firmly in their place. People who were too friendly with staff were simply afraid of them. And where would be the sense in that.

Coffee was brought and the port. And still Admiral Barry rambled on under the genial misapprehension that he was helping to keep the party going while Rory gazed back at him with the solemnity of the half-drunk. 'I'm afraid I cannot agree with you, Admiral' he said. 'Not wholly anyway. We have to consider _why_ these men decided to rise in revolt. For they thought they had reason, you know. They didn't want to get themselves shot for nothing.'

The Admiral bridled. 'Pro-Germans!' he barked. 'Every last one of them in the Kaiser's pay. Mister Dillon said so in the House of Commons and I agree with him.'

Rory smiled a very slow and menacing smile which reminded his mother of her own father on one of his bad days. 'May I suggest, Admiral' he said silkily. 'That possibly neither Mister Dillon or even your very good self knows anything at all about the matter. I have no wish to offend you, sir' causing the most grievous offence by implying that a whippersnapper of no more than twenty-five years could ever be in a position to offer offence to an eighty-year old who had served three sovereigns. 'But I think that we are all inclined to imagine that what we think must be what everyone else thinks.' He screwed himself round on his elbow and looked to where the Admiral was trying to contain himself lest he should commit the unpardonable offence of being rude to a man at his own table. 'Tell me, Admiral, if you don't mind, of course. What do you know about the rebellion? Of your own knowledge I mean. Who were the leaders and who were executed? How many men did the rebels have and how were they armed? I'm sure you will have all the information at your fingertips.'

'Rory!' interrupted his mother, scandalised. Such things simply were not done.

The Admiral addressed his cigar, carefully piercing it with one match and using another match to warm the end before actually lighting it. The Admiral always made great play about lighting his cigar - cheroot really; he said he had acquired the habit on the China station and could not smoke anything else now. Then he said, almost casually, 'Well, there was Connolly, the Labour fellow. And Pearse...' His voice tailed away in indecision.

'Connolly and Pearse!' sneered Rory, half rising in his seat. 'Connolly and Pearse? Only Connolly and Pearse? There were sixteen of them. Just imagine that. Sixteen men shot to death for fighting for their own country. Anyone down in the village could recite their names without even thinking about it. Sixteen good, ordinary men...'

'Sixteen traitors' snorted the Admiral. Lavinia compressed her lips and the Laceys looked uncomfortable but knew they could not decently do anything about leaving yet. Constance's eyes flashed hatred at her husband's younger brother but she too shut her mouth in a hard line for it would never do to make a scene before guests. The nerve of it. Defending men everyone knew were German agents trying to prevent decent Irishmen doing their duty as poor dear Andrew had. God, Rory, she thought. You will pay for this some day, not seeing in the young-old face that the man had already paid as much as he could.

'Good ordinary men, begging your pardon, Admiral' Rory insisted. 'I do not say they were right but I do say they were entitled to their opinion as much as the rest of us.' His voice rose as his mother prayed uncharacteristically for something to happen -a storm, anything - to end what seemed to be the most embarrassing scene she had ever been involved in. Wherever had he got his strange ideas from? And surely he would realise that a woman in her state of health deserved all the consideration he could give. Andrew would, she told herself. Andrew would do anything rather than hurt his mother. The wraith of her own hardriding father seemed to hover above Rory's chair and it was almost as if she could hear his voice reiterating relentlessly the logic of the matter as he saw it. Never before had she know who Rory took after. Now that she did a frisson of fear passed through her like a cold draught and she shivered.

'Are you all right, Lavinia?' asked Constance, rising in her seat only to be waved down again. It was, she thought, typical that Rory should not see the distress he was causing his mother. Not to say herself. After all it was her husband who was killed in France, her husband she could now see seated at the head of the table. She was the widow. Biting her lips so hard it hurt she politely asked if anyone wanted more coffee and the Laceys seized the opportunity to break the tension which had from nothing become almost palpable.

No, thank you. Lavinia would not have more coffee and neither would the Admiral who like most small men had a ferocious temper and a low boiling point. What the blasted boy was getting at he could not even guess. He sounded almost like one of those Sinn Feiners they used to have in Dublin. But he couldn't be one of them. Not an Aylmer. Not Archie Aylmer's son.

'I do not say they were right' Rory repeated. 'But I do say they were entitled to think they were right. And they most certainly were not in the pay of Germany. That is the most foul lie any British government ever perpetrated and they have perpetrated a few in their time. We used to talk about it in the Mess' he explained. 'All the brigade officers. Dublins, Leinsters, Munsters, South Irish Horse, all the Irish regiments. All of us thought the rebels had some right on their side...'

'Traitors!' hissed Constance suddenly. 'Traitors. They deserved to be shot.'

Rory eyed her as if she might be a stranger. 'You think so, do you? You really think so? And how could they be traitors? They were not Englishmen. It was not their country which was at war with Germany..' He too stopped and grinned apologetically. 'I'm running off the handle' he explained ruefully. 'Be much better if I kept my mouth shut.'

'It would indeed, young man' said the Admiral unwisely. 'Have you forgotten your own brother, at whose table we sit now, gave his life on the Somme for King and Empire?'

Rory brushed his hand wearily across his face. 'So did Tom Kettle' he said. 'And Francis Ledwidge. And hundreds - thousands -more. Gincy. Gallipoli. The Marne. It makes no difference. They all died for something they thought worth dying for but it wasn't anyone's empire, I'm sure of that. Tom Kettle was an out and out Sinn Feiner' he added. 'Did you know that? Tom Kettle was an Irish nationalist just like Pearse and Connolly and all the rest of them. Dublin man. Drumcondra I think. Used to talk about it a lot. I learned a great deal from Major Dalton. For one thing I learned who and what I was, not a make-believe Englishman but an Irishman who happens to like England. Why I don't rightly know. Expect it's in the blood somewhere.'

He gestured impatiently for the decanter to be passed again and when he filled his glass the port came up to the rim and trembled there as if it might overflow while he gave it his most

31

serious consideration. The Admiral snorted and fell to studying the inch-long ash adhering to the end of his cheroot. The Rector cleared his throat preparatory to pouring oil on the most troubled waters he had seen for many a year and Lacey pulled out his thin gold evening watch and made a pretence of being surprised at the time.

'You see' said Rory placing the palms of both hands flat on the table. 'We never try to get it right in our minds. We think of ourselves as English when we are whether we like it or not as Irish as anyone down in Gorteen. That's the way the British think of us. They don't think of us as being British. They only think of us as being Irish, good men in a fight and hard drinkers and riders. They like our whim-sic-al-ity' he said with a little slurring of the word. 'Our whim-sic-al-ity' he repeated as if the expression pleased him. 'We are their licensed jesters and they love us because we admire them so much. I tell you' he continued with raised forefinger pointing to each in turn. 'If every one of us here lives to be a thousand we still will not be considered as equals by the English. And do you want to know why? I'll tell you'. It's because the English believe - they truly and honestly believe and there isn't a race of people anywhere I admire more - they quite sincerely believe no other race is their equal. They think it natural they should rule Ireland. And I'll tell you another thing, we think it natural too.' He waved his hand extravagantly. 'But that's all going to change. Who says so? Emmet Dalton says so and so does every officer and man of the Dublins, the Munsters, the Leinsters, the Rangers and the South Irish Horse. Even the Inniskillings. Ireland unfree shall never be at rest.' He looked at the dark red pool spreading from his overturned glass. 'Did I do that?' he asked. 'Did I knock that glass over? Well, never mind. There's more port in the decanter. Give it a fair wind, please.

'If you will kindly excuse me' said his mother coldly as she rose to her feet and reached for the support of Constance's arm. The company stood as the Rector hurried to offer his help and the Laceys murmured something about a very nice evening and being glad to see Rory back again but they would really

32

have to be going while the Admiral gazed with undisguised contempt on a man who shamed the King's uniform and was glad his father was not there to see it. Horsewhipped him, Archie would.

'Will there be anything else, Master Rory?' asked Nellie Walker, making herself very busy with tray and crumb brush. 'Mrs Watkins is helping your mother to her bed and I don't think the rest of the company will be coming back to table. But if I can get you anything else, more coffee maybe or another bottle of port, I'd be honoured to oblige.'

'No, thanks, Nellie' he answered, surveying the wreckage of his homecoming dinner and thinking that things could never be the same again for he had committed the unforgivable sin of criticising the country whose perfection was the only real justification for their own existence in a land where they were neither native or alien, where men who doffed their caps respectfully looked on them with inimical eyes and laughed with a bitter sound when they were almost out of earshot. 'No, thanks, Nellie' he said again. 'I rather think I've had enough for one evening. Maybe too much.'

Next morning Constance and Rory met at breakfast, Lavinia as usual having her meal from a tray in her room. Wicklow was playing one of her enchanting tricks with the sun slanting in brilliant gold down the hillside to illuminate and pick out the greens and greys of rocks and plants and leaving pockets of velvet-soft mist in the lowest hollows while the air was strong enough to go to a man's head if he was not used to it.

Constance greeted him coldly as Nellie set a big bowl of thick porridge floating in yellow cream before him. When the girl had gone she said in a distant voice 'I hope you will have the grace to apologise to your mother this morning.'

Rory looked over the heavy silver spoon which held the porridge as a spade holds earth and answered 'Of course I shall. It was unforgivable of me to ruin her dinner party the way I did. But I wasn't drunk you know. I knew what I was saying. And I meant it. I still do' He gestured through the window towards Knocknagowna with the two Sugarloafs beyond faerylike in the misty magic of the day. 'That isn't Devon or Cornwall out there and it isn't Scotland or Wales either. It's Wicklow. Ireland. Where we have lived all our lives, and our fathers and our father's fathers before us. We couldn't be English even if we wanted to, so we shouldn't try.'

Still unappeased she said 'And maybe you will feel inclined to apologise to me also.'

He looked amazed and swallowed hastily. 'I didn't say anything to offend you, did I?'

She said bitterly 'You as good as compared Andrew with those criminals.'

Again amazed he asked 'What criminals?'

'You know' she said. 'The rebels. The 1916 lot. You implied there wasn't much difference between them.'

Angered, he exploded. 'They were not criminals. They were good patriotic men just like Andrew. They had a different loyalty, that's all.' He laid down his spoon and spoke very earnestly. 'Constance. We all have to come to terms with life as it is now. I know you miss Andrew badly and I miss him too, more than you and mother will ever guess. When I was a boy Andrew was my adored big brother and when he was killed I thought it my duty to go and take his place in his memory. That was when I started learning about myself, who I was and where I came from. I have half a notion Andrew must have learned it too. Kettle, Ledwidge and that lot, what used to be called Redmond's Volunteers, they didn't go to war just to free poor little Belgium. They also went to war to free poor little Ireland. For no one likes being a member of a subject race. We all want to be ruled by our own kind...'

'We are their own kind' she interjected. 'We are as Irish as they are.'

'How can you possibly say that?' he asked wearily. 'For the hundreds of years we've been here we know nothing about the people. We know practically nothing about their lives and nothing at all about the way they feel and think. As far as we are concerned they might well be an alien race speaking a language we do not understand.' He pushed his plate aside and reached for a slice of buttered turnover while Constance lifted the teapot to pour him a cup. 'Constance' he said hesitatingly, 'I've never mentioned Andrew to you because I know how it upsets you. But I share your grief. We all do. But grief is a very personal, very private thing. What you and I and mother feel for Andrew is exactly the same as every other wife, brother and mother feels for every man killed in war be he rebel or German or anything else. Because death is death and that's all there is to it. But we have to learn if we are to survive. What happened in 1916 can't be stopped now however much we ignore it. Dalton and that lot, all the men I met in France, expects England to concede Home Rule now in return for Andrew and all the other Irishmen who gave their lives. It isn't too much to ask, is it? If Home Rule doesn't come now after all the promises there will be real warfare in this country. Then we will all have to make up our minds where we stand.'

'There is no doubt where you would stand' she said contemptuously.

'I don't know' he answered, passing his hand across his face in a characteristic gesture she could remember in Andrew. The remembrance shocked her for she had never before seen any similarity between the brothers. Now that her attention had been drawn to it there were too many not to have been noticed if the had been interested enough. The broad forehead and the stubby jawline were the same and they had the same grey-green eyes. And if she had ever had cause to speak to Andrew in the same circumstances she felt sure his reactions would have been the same although Andrew was always too much the gentleman ever to give offence to anyone, not even obliquely.

She heard Rory say 'I suppose it would depend on how things were at the time. Those men in France, Dalton and that lot, Ernie Crawford and his crowd, they have as much right to think of themselves as British as anyone here. But they don't. They think of themselves as Irish and we will just have to make up our minds what we are before someone tells us. It's not going to be easy, Constance. But somehow we have to accept our Irishness and live with it.'

She said anxiously 'I hope you are not going to say anything of this to Lavinia.' He assured her that was the last thing he would wish to do though he was privately resolved to stand his ground when the time came for the sake of the men left in unmarked graves in France. What was left of them anyway for the rats did not leave a dead body intact for long. A memory of the trenches and shellholes of the battlefield with their grotesquely sprawling corpses feeding vermin big as puppies flashed through his mind. Constance sensed a resolution which had never been in poor dear Andrew. To steer the conversation into safer channels she asked 'What did you think of Miss Lacey?'

With an effort he wrenched his thoughts away from a nightmare he had never expected to live through. 'She seems to be very nice' he answered, trying to remember what the girl had actually been like. 'Why?'

'I just wondered' Constance answered. 'I thought that maybe Lavinia had invited them for a purpose. You will soon have to be thinking about getting married, Rory. Ardnagoilte needs a mistress.'

Impulsively he answered 'Ardnagoilte has a mistress. You. Two I expect if truth be told. The thought of marriage has never entered my head.' He was going to say that there were more important things in life than marriage, but that might have been indelicate. 'I have to find out what has been happening on the estate since I went away. I shall be looking to you to steer me in the right direction.'

'I was thinking of going back to Roscommon' she said and he told her almost angrily that there was no question of that. 'This is as much you home as mine now. Besides, Lavinia obviously depends on you. Unless you very much want to go we would all be much happier if you stayed here.'

Although she was pleased Constance did not very much like the prospect of having Lavinia as a daily diet for dear knows how many years ahead. But to be a widow in Roscommon would be just as bad as being a widow in Wicklow. There was much to be thought of. As Maggie hovered waiting to clear the table Constance asked 'What had you in mind for today?' The hunt meets at Carrowmore at nine and the horses need exercise.'

He thought about it a few seconds. Then he said 'I rather think not. One of our lads lives at Rathmore. I think I will ride across and see what he thinks of things now. Chances are he will have me for lunch so I will not see you before dinner this evening. And thanks for being so understanding with mother. I know it has been bad for you but it must be that much worse for her because she is on the short end of living now. Having you in the house must be a great comfort to her.' Then 'Maggie. What papers do we have delivered?'

'I think only the Irish Times, sir.'

'Well from now on I want to see all the Irish papers, including the Freeman's Journal. Ask Skoiles to put them on order, will you, please.'

The girl said she would, thinking with horror what the old master would have said if anyone ever dared introduce the Freeman's Journal into his house. It did not bearing thinking of.

When the Widow Mangan described her home as being no more than a wee bit of a tigeen she was for once not exaggerating. Even by Irish terms it hardly merited the description of a cottage which were in the main sturdily constructed of bricks and mortar with something in the nature of a lavatory within easy reach of the back door and maybe a shed big enough to accommodate a pig or two.

Of course such palaces would be in the village proper while the widow Mangan's hovel of a home lay outside on the rough road which led through rioting rhododendrons and headhigh cowparsley to the great iron gates of Ardnagoilte with eroding lions atop each gatepost and the snug lodgehouse which no Catholic could ever hope to occupy for it was only in nature that a Protestant landowner should want his portals guarded by a fellow Protestant. Not that the portals could be said to be guarded by old Mrs Whitmore but when Bill Whitmore breathed his last at Gallipoli his widow and her family became a charge on the honour of the Aylmers. And anyway as far as Gorteen was concerned the gates of the big house could remain open forever for there were none outside to wish them ill.

Yet when the coachpainted dog-cart pulled up in the lane with Herself sitting painfully erect on the seat the widow Mangan asked all the saints forgiveness for the wicked things she had been thinking of the decent woman who was going to tell her when the men would be around to fix the thatch.

But divil a thatch was in it. As the widow furtively wiped her hands on her filthy pinafore and leered frighteningly through her toothless mouth Mrs Aylmer said, unexpectedly and abruptly, for one did not waste niceties on villagers, 'Your eldest girl, Mrs Mangan, Eileen, I think.'

Mystified, Lizzie agreed that her eldest girl was indeed named Eileen.

'She will be leaving school soon' said Mrs Aylmer.

'Next month' Lizzie Mangan agreed and waited to hear what it was all about.

'When she does send her up to the house and I will start her in the kitchen helping Mrs Comiskey' said the good Mrs Aylmer, touching the pony's rump with her whip and trundling sedately away thinking that almost the last thing she wanted was another Gorteen girl in her kitchen, stupid and dirty creatures that they were. But the Mangans needed the money and one had a Christian duty to do whatever one could to help the less fortunate.

It was a few minutes before Lizzie stopped swearing under her breath and weeks before she became used to the terrible insult offered to her and her family. Send her up to the house indeed! Like some fecking beggar girl. Her that was the best looking and most liked girl in the barony. As a miser hoards his treasure Lizzie added this latest affront to the many already cherished against the inevitable day of reckoning when all who dared scorn the princely Mangans would themselves be humbled to the dust. Which was almost the only thing which

made life in Gorteen endurable. That and the children. Fo.
trouble and all that they were, her six children were all that
justified her own existence.

So it was with something less than cordiality that the looked
up from the pot when the door opened and a walking scarecrow
stepped into the little room. 'God save all here' said the
apparition, beaming the goodwill which is the beggar's stock
in trade at the children - Larry, Eileen, Rosie, Imelda, Lily and
Bernadette - eating their meal of egg and fried bread at the
table.

Lizzie thought that wasn't it a quare thing oul' Shawneen
always appeared at dinner time and Biddy Horrigan said it
was always tea time with the rashers already in the pan when
he called on her, which left him only with breakfast to get from
somewhere else for he had the look of a man who seldom went
hungry with the big red face of him and his body thick and
well nourished under the rags he called his clothes. But she
knew that we all have a duty to feed God's poor and to have
refused the beggarman might have brought bad luck on the
house. And it was the law of the tribe never to turn a stranger
from your door. Not that oul' Shawneen could be called a
stranger. In a manner of speaking you could set the clock by
him and it would never do to give him anything to tell at other
people's tables.

'God save you kindly, Shawneen' she answered. 'Will you
take a bite with us itself?'

'That I will and right gladly, Mrs Mangan' replied the tramp,
edging his way on the wooden form and jamming his thigh
against the swarthy Eileen who, quite unnoticed by her mother,
had started to be a woman with the sort of figure a man might
get married for. At the far end of the form Larry dug his heel
into the earth floor and muttered something unkind under his
breath. 'It's a tidy step from Stillorgan' ended the tramp,
beaming at the children who gazed stonily back.

Resignedly Mrs Mangan placed her own plate of food before
him and, as a hostess always must, proceeded to put him at
his ease.' That's a tidy step alright' she said. 'An' where've ya

been this time, Shawneen?'

'Dubelin a course' he answered indignantly. 'Dubelin, Wickla, Kildare, Dubelin. The same sorry pilgrimage I've hadta make since the redcoats burned me poor oul' father's house over his head an' turned us all out on the road, bad cess ta thim!' The egg and fried bread were already gone but the taypot looked like there might be another cup or two on it and anyway he couldn't just ate up an' be off like somewan never had no manners. 'Dubelin, Wickla, Kildare, Dubelin' he repeated. 'On the road all weathers day an' night without rest nor cease, all the time smellin' the timbers've me own fine home smoulderin' and the pigeens squealin' an' the oul' dog barkin' his last like it was a Christian perishin' in the flames. Ten acres we had, Mrs Mangan...'

Lizzie knew that. Everyone knew that although not all were disposed to believe it, for every man who took to the road had a heartbreaking story to tell and God alone knows everywan has their own trouble so they have.

But it would have been unmannerly to doubt him. 'An did ya see annywan in Dubelin?' asked Lizzie, still the good hostess, still anxious to put her uninvited guest at ease for it was a well-known fact that travelling' people could put curses on anyone who did not treat them as they should. And there was enough trouble in life without looking for any more. She poured the beggar a mug of tea and watched him ladling sugar into it as if the cupboard was full to overflowing.

Shawneen blew on the mug and raised it to his lips. 'Did I see annywan?' he asked rhetorically. 'Did I see annywan in Dubelin? <u>Only</u> the vic-er-oy hisself' and waited to hear their gasps of astonishment. None came. The children had not the slightest notion what a viceroy might be and to their mother it was no more than a word she heard occasionally. Again as a matter of manners she said 'Is that a fact, Shawneen?'

'As true as I'm sittin' here at this table. Goin' down Dame Street in a grand carriage he was, with sojers before him an' sojers behind him and sojers on each side of him an' all his orders.'

'An what class've a man is he?' asked Lizzie. Though she did not know what a viceroy was she knew that it was someone high up, wann've the Upper Ten in a manner of speaking.

Shawneen settled his elbows on the table, wondering if there might be another egg in the house or if maybe the oul' widda would fry him another coupla pieces of bread. But the man of the roads must pay for his supper one way or another and if it was talk she wanted then talk he would give her and think himself lucky she wasn't wanna the gamey wans.

'Well now, Mrs Mangan' he said. 'That's a question I do often be askin' myself. I mane, ya hear Giniril Lord This an' Giniril Lord That an' in yer minds eye ya see a big hansome man like it could be Cookelin or Finn Mack Oole. An' at the heela the reel what is it but a pot-bellied little man with a bitta glass stuck in his eye like somethin' y'd see in the thee-ay-thur. It's a wonder ta me they let the people see them like that. I mane, it's very hard ta feel respect fer a man looks like a playactor so it is. But we'll see it no longer if I'm anny judge a things. There's talk in Dubelin've a new fella, some fella called Collins from the bogs somewhere, Cork I think. An' from what I hear it's him that'll be knockin' the glass outa their eye an' that before they're a lot older. Dubelin is fulla him. Right an' left everywhere ya go people is talkin' about how he's gointo drive the Saxon out wance an' fer all.'

'Ah that'll be when the Seven Captains come' said the widow, thinking that she didn't care much who or what was the vice-er-oy if only somewan would get her roof rethatched. She very much doubted that any Corkman was going to do it for they were very well known for taking care of their own. Bad as the Prodestans they were.

Shawneen, recognising that his chances of getting more to eat in this place were very slim and that he was wasting his news on a lot of Wicklow goatsuckers, took his leave with effusive thanks and calling every blessing possible on the widow and her house. Then he headed south in the hope of reaching a place he knew outside Gorey where he was certain they would find something for a man who hadn't broken his fast since daybreak.

Larry whined 'Sure I don't know why ya let that oul' eejit in the house at all, Mammy, ta ate up yer dinner an' stink up the place like a mungery dog, so I don't.'

She rounded on him. 'That man' she said. 'Is a direct descendent from Phelim MacFeagh an' if he had his rights it's Kinga Wickla he'd be today. He does us great honour eatin' at our table an' if ya don't get yerself outside an' chop a few sticks it's the weight've me hand y'll be feelin' an' that before yer much older.'

Larry went sulkily, knowing his mother would never raise her hand to the boy of the family although his sisters felt it often enough. But then they were only gerrls.

Lizzie wondered if oul' Shawneen could possibly be right, if she would live to see the day the arrogant Aylmers were put out on the road and all their riches shared among the more deserving poor. It did not seem really likely but it was a nice thing to be thinking of while she was toilin' an' moilin' to put a bit of food in the childer's mouths. And Larry was right in one thing. Oul' Shawneen did smell like a mungery dog. She whisked the dirt from one place to another and felt herself to be infinitely superior to a man without a home to call his own. 'Eileen, acushla' she said. 'How would ya like to work up at the big house? If I talk ta Missus Aylmer maybe she'd let ya start in the kitchen. Y'd get yer food annyway an' that'd be a big help ta me for I don't know where ta turn fer the best so I don't.'

Eileen started crying. The big house was as a foreign land to her and she didn't want to have to work among a lot of Prodestans so she didn't. But already she was gaining stature in the eyes of her family and she could see herself coming home every day laden with good things for them to eat. And Seamus Fogarty worked in the stables there, so maybe he'd marry her and give her a home of her own and children with ears to be boxed whenever she felt the need to. Life at the big house might not be so bad after all.

42

One beggar had been given a few coppers from the pile on the hall table and another had been sent away with a flea in his ear for coming a week before he was expected. A woman from the glens without a shoe to her feet had her offering of a shilling for a Mass for the soul of her deceased husband thrust back at her with a bitter injunction that 'The men in this house don't say Mass for buttons' and departed with a thousand apologies for disturbing the person next in sanctity to the priest himself by lifting the brass knocker while Julia Begley was immersed in the back pages of Peg's Paper where there did be some quare oul' letters to be sure and she with a day's work behind her. If the word got round that the Parish Priest was a soft touch you'd never see the last of them from one days end to another.

She opened the damper on the range and lifted her skirt to let the heat get to where it would do the most good, wondered if she would make herself another pot of tea and then decided it was too near bedtime. So, and as she often did, she thought complacently of her life as housekeeper to the Parish Priest of Gorteen. And she could not find a thing in it which was not wholly to her liking.

God had been to Julia Begley. Not that she had not been good to Him in her own way, taking the best of care of God's Anointed year in year out and seeing to it that the ragtag and bobtail of the parish did not distract the dear man from his sacred office. At this moment she wanted for nothing and would not have changed placed with any woman in the five provinces. Let the weather do its worst outside, here in the stuccoed presbytery everything was cosy and warm. And it would be the same tomorrow and the day after and the day after that again until the Lord chose to call her to her heavenly reward for the faithful daughter of the Church she had always been.

The truth was that Father Peter would be lost without her. She did not need anyone to tell her that. Over twenty-five years had flown since first she took employment with the young curate of Carriglee but it seemed no more than days since she left her own father's cottage on the steep side of Maumtrasna in bleak Mayo and found her way by a succession of parishes good and bad to this fine house and a position in life only a step below that of the reverend father himself. People in Gorteen respected Julia Begley. To her face. What they did behind her back did not bother her a thrawneen for it was always them that had to come to her and never her who had to go to them.

As the good coal flames flickered in the grate she counted her many blessings. Like an oul' married couple they were except that he wouldn't dare enter her kitchen without permission and he didn't come tapping on her door any more, for they were both getting on in years and them days were past. Less fortunate women had to get married for their living with husbands who knocked them about and families more trouble than they were worth, but a priest's housekeeper got the best of both words: she enjoyed all the privileges of marriage without any of its responsibilities. She had an assured living and social position into the bargain and she would never want for money for every penny he ever paid her was lying in the bank gathering interest as the years passed by. And wasn't that a wonderful system? You just put your bit of money in the bank and the bank added to it each and every year it lay there while you lived well on the housekeeping.

Again she wondered about the tea but if she did she would be up in the night so she'd have a glass of hot milk instead with maybe a dropeen of the priest's whiskey from the end of the last bottle.

In the parlour the old priest Father Gilligan relaxed before a roaring fire with a glass of whiskey to hand and a copy of yesterday's Independent delivered by Jerry Madigan, the constable, who picked it up for him every day from the train at Arklow. A good man was Madigan. Do anything for anybody. Pick up a doctor's note in the morning and go miles out of his way to deliver the medicine that same night, standing on his pedals to breast the hills which encircled Gorteen on every side. Nothing was too much trouble for Madigan and he was strict in his observation of his religious duties, which was more than

44

could be said for many a one around here.

The priest sighed at the iniquities of a small place like Gorteen where evil ought to have been unknown. He relit his old briar pipe and wondered what the world was coming to when slips of gerrls hardly out of school whispered confidences in the darkness of the confessional that would have sent their parents brokenhearted to their graves if only they knew of them. It was a relief to hear the 'cursing' and 'inattention at Mass' of the older people. He wondered if it had always been that way or if he had only become aware of it lately. For the truth was that he hardly ever listened closely to a confession and absolved all sinners on the assumption that they must be truly penitent to come to confession in the first place.

Of course he had a greater duty but a man had to be practical. Most of them seemed to think that the Church and its sacraments existed for their own convenience and they would have to bear the consequences on the fatal day of judgement. If a gerrl got into real trouble he would try to bring the culprit to the altar, but it seldom came to that. Usually the gerrl took herself off to England to work in a hospital or something and if they ever showed their face in Gorteen again it would be as a brazen hussy in cheap finery and fearing neither God nor man and then he would pray for them in an agony of remorse for having failed his duty as he saw it. For himself it was a great blessing that the days of sinning were over or he would have to be making his own confession to the bumptious O'Reilly or cycling all the way to Father Brannan at Gortmore and that was a long way to go to atone for what was no more than a moments weakness.

He sipped his whiskey and opened the newspaper. Then he started in his armchair with the new-lit pipe almost falling from his mouth when he saw the headline on the front page. In some place called Soloheadbeg in Tipperary two unarmed policemen had been gunned down in broad daylight as they walked beside a cart of dynamite for the nearby quarry. The blood ran cold in his veins. Two policeman. Both of them Catholics. Blasted off the face of the earth by men who were undoubtedly Catholics themselves for there wasn't much of the other kind in Tipperary. What in the sacred name of God was the country coming to when Catholic shot Catholic even when protected by the uniform of the RIC?

A foreboding of evil passed through him and he gulped a stiff slug of whiskey as he remembered that all this had happened before, not in his own time but in his father's time. And many a tale he had to tell of the United Irishmen, the Fenians they called themselves, and how they set out to destroy the blessed peace of holy Ireland in the perverted cause of a freedom which no one was bothered about. But Tipperary was a comfortable distance from Wicklow and they would never have that shame to endure in Gorteen, please God.

O'Reilly, he thought. Father Eugene O'Reilly would be making excuses for the killers. But there was no excusing murder. Even the British did not attempt to excuse murder. And no Catholic should ever send another to face his Maker unconfessed. Somehow to him that seemed to be the very worst of it.

For weeks on end a fine rain filled the valley edge to edge and made every tussock of sedge grass a heavy laden sponge. Usually trickling rills foamed in spate and the very rocks wept great dripping tears as if kindness had gone from the land forever. Clouds shrouded Knocknagowna and all of Gorteen kept indoors as much as it could. It was the worst Christmastide anyone could remember. 1920 came in with veils of eddying rain but occasionally a brilliant shaft of sunlight penetrated the gloom to bring the message that all would still be well, apple blossom would bloom again and the corn would stand upright when spring had chased winter away to wherever it had come from.

Rory Aylmer trudged the road into the village to stretch his legs and his mind away from the claustrophobia of the house. Big as it was the house still had walls and kin as they were he needed to be away from his mother and Constance to think clearly what he should do with the life which the old gods had preserved to him even as they snatched it away from others.

46

For war is a terrible thing and Rory had come through the most terrible of wars ever known. Now that the smells and the sounds of battle had receded almost beyond recall he was aware that life is too precious to be squandered aimlessly and that he needed to make the greatest possible use of the years which were left to him.

Constance was somewhere just under the surface of his thinking. Between them had grown a bond which was more than affection and less than love, born of their common concern for Lavinia and the estate on which subject his brother's widow had proved to be remarkably knowledgeable for a woman who had grown up in a male dominated household.

That all was well with Ardnagoilte was a comforting thing to know, but there still were problems. If Andrew had made a will on marriage no one had yet found it and until someone did Constance's portion had to be assumed. The actual estate was entailed on Rory but the stocks and shares which had passed from their father to Andrew might be anyone's and whoever ran Ardnagoilte needed money behind him, so the whole business was up in the air and likely to remain so for quite some time. And he wondered how matters would stand when Ireland was granted Home Rule as she undoubtedly would, for not even the most callous of governments could go back on it's given word. Irish rule in Ireland seemed to be only reasonable but he wondered just how far it would go and if the Roman Catholic Church would be able to keep its fingers ;out of the till for nothing excited the grey men like the smell of money. So his father had always said and he must have known what he was talking about.

Home Rule. A green flag with a golden harp on it flying over every public building in the land. Somehow he did not relish the idea very much. And then what? It was difficult to see a government in the Irish Party at Westminster. But who else was there? And what would happen to the landowners and their estates? What would happen to Ardnagoilte?

To hell with it all! There was a tumbledown shed just off the road where they used to stock winter feed for the animals. He

47

would smoke a pipe or two there and maybe clear his thinking. Be out of the rain anyway. For he hadn't a dog's chance of lighting a pipe in the open.

Inside the shed was dry as a bone with not even a trace of wet on the pounded earth floor. Against the half-light of the lowering day a darker shadow crouched over a small pile of smouldering oak chips, coaxing it into a flame.

Rory stepped through the door-space. 'Hello, there!' he said and the figure answered 'Hello yerself!' before turning to show a flashily handsome face with more than a trace of arrogance in it, a sensuous mouth and eyes like onyx, the whole topped by wiry black hair bejewelled with raindrops. The eyes hardened. 'Hello, Misthur Aylmer!' he amended. 'Sure it's a bad oul' day that in it' as he thought privately so that's what young Aylmer looks like nowadays. Well, the war hadn't done him much harm as far as appearances went anyway. He'd never had to go short of anything in his life, not like poor Paddy Boucher from Rathnew. While this young bucko had been striding around like God almighty with a proper gas mask strapped to his chest, fellas like Paddy had just been told to pee in their handkerchiefs and hold that over their face when the yellow fog wafted across the battlefield.

Broken in health at the age of thirty Paddy might be but he could still shoot a gun and soon they would all be knowing about it. For the word from HQ was that anyone who had been in the service of the English crown might be a spy and so a legitimate target in the fight for the liberation of a country which still had too many khaki pups prancin' and struttin' over other people's land. Just look at this fella in his fine officer's trenchcoat with leather leggings and good leather soles half an inch thick to his boots, lazily filling a pipe and looking at himself like he was dirt beneath his feet. Well, not for much longer. Seeing that the 'Young Master' had no idea at all who he was talking to he offered 'Derry Keogh. Though there's some call me Darkie. Because've me hair, I expect. I work on the place. Misthur Nolan took me on when oul' Sinnott died.'

It was another shock for Rory. Old Micky Sinnott dead! Micky of the short leg and the twisted grin whose reaction to every calamity was always to say that it might have been worse although what could be worse than going through life from boyhood with a deformity like his Rory could never imagine. But, Sinnott dead! And he did not know because no one had told him. Maybe they did not even know it at the house or had forgotten someone as insignificant as poor old Micky Sinnott who could calm the most fractious horse by breathing into its nostrils and whispering secret words into its ear. He himself had not even noticed that Micky was no longer around the place. And that made him as bad as anyone else.

He said 'I didn't know. I'm sorry' and when a painful gap began to yawn between them he said too politely 'I hope you like Gorteen.'

'Faith an' I should!' retorted Keogh with a trace of bitterness. 'Seein' that I was born an' raised here, baptised be oul' Father Pethur hisself an' got me learning' in the very school yer own father built.' It was as if the man was being deliberately insolent but not in any way which could easily be identified.

Rory said, anxious for some reason to win Keogh's good opinion and because it was on his mind too much lately 'What do you think of Home Rule, Keogh?' quite unaware that he was turning a very rusty knife in a still suppurating wound by addressing the man by his surname. To be called 'Dermot' or 'Derry' or even 'Darkie' would have been quite bad enough but tolerable. To be referred to only as 'Keogh' set the dark man's teeth on edge because it was a peculiarly English practice.

'It's not Home Rule we're wantin', Misthur Aylmer' he replied viciously. Rory wondered if indeed that was what most working people felt on the subject. In which case both his mother and Constance would be quite right when they said that all the villagers wanted was something to eat and a place to sleep and that things like bathrooms and proper lavatories would only make them feel uncomfortable, while self-government was the very least of their concerns. Maybe that was what Westminster thought too for it was hardly ever mentioned even in the Irish papers now. There would be no green flags with golden harps on them for many a year yet and that made him feel somehow sad. It was shabby of Britain to go back on its word yet again. He felt very young and very callow as he watched Keogh swinging out of the hut with a laconic 'take care' before he stepped out into the still swirling rain.

It seemed such a pity. Ireland could rule itself and Ireland should rule itself as Lloyd George had promised. The Irish understood their own problems better than anyone in faraway Whitehall could ever know. Ireland had doctors, lawyers, writers and academics. Some of the politicians were sound and the civil service was almost wholly Irish. Between them they ought to be able to govern an easy-going and good-tempered people if only England would give them the chance. And this time England should not renege on its promise for that brought shame to all of its people.

Breasting unconcernedly into the relenting rain Derry Keogh thought 'Well, he got his answer there all right. Home Rule is it? Maybe Home Rule was good enough for the likes of Griffith and that lot but for this generation nothing less than a republic would do. And if they had to slaughter every Ascendancy cur in the country to get it so much the better. Beat them first and then send them packing.'

Larry Mangan had been haunting the dairy ever since the news of Rory's return had spread through the village.

Days, weeks, months, the outcome would always be the same. Larry would say 'Can I see Master Rory, please?' and the dairyman would snort and ask what the likes of him would be wanting with <u>Mister</u> Rory. When Larry explained that they were friends the dairyman would sniff disdainfully and tell him to be off before he set the dog on him while Larry found comfort in imagining what Rory would to the dairyman when he heard the way he treated his best friend. At the very least the man would be out on this ear bag and baggage and at best Rory would fell him with one blow first and Larry hoped he

50

would be there when it happened.

They actually met one day when Rory was setting out to ride the bounds of the estate. Guiding the sturdy cob through a thicket of rhododendron bushes by the south wall he found himself suddenly confronted by an overjoyed ragamuffin who greeted him with an enthusiastic 'Hello, Rory!' At first he did not recognise the gangling lad in one of his own Old Wesley blazers with his rawboned wrists protruding a full four inches. Then he remembered. 'Hello, Mangan' he answered and touched the cob with his heel to keep it moving.

To Larry it was like a slap in the face. For more than a year they had been Larry and Rory, barefoot in the river of scrambling the hill to pick wild strawberries. Now he was Mangan. Just Mangan. His childish face contorted with pain. 'I was at the Den yesterday' he said as if it was of some importance.

Rory wondered. The Den? Oh, yes. A rabbit infested hollow beneath overhanging branches of elder. It was a secret place, the Lord alone knew why for no one had ever come looking for them. What did they do there? Nothing much. Eat bread and jam sandwiches and laugh a lot, what at he could not now imagine. He remembered he used to wheedle the bread and jam from cook and that she always complained because he wanted so much. But he could do anything with cook. Still could. It was a very long time ago.

The agonised face was turned to him again. 'I thought maybe we could tickle a trout or catch a few collickers...'

Rory had almost forgotten the freshwater crabs which were good for nothing as far as he knew. Catching them had been the whole object of the exercise and they would fasten their greeny claws into anything which floated before them. Collickers. The very word belong to the childhood he left behind when he went to Dublin to enlist. But he supposed lads must still be catching them in the still water below the bridge on days when the sun seemed always to shine and heather-fat bees buzzed about their business.

'What was the war like, Rory?'

51

'The war? ' He answered only because he could not decently do otherwise. 'Oh, wet mostly. Mud and rain. Not really very nice.'

Larry fixed him with his eyes and asked intensely 'Did you ever kill a German?' and Rory said not that he knew of, that war wasn't like that really, not like it seems to be in books. 'You seldom see the man you're firing at. Mostly its shells coming over and as long as you stay in the trench you're safe enough. It's only when you have to go over the top you stand a chance of being hit. But it wasn't all that bad', remembering mess nights drinking harsh young brandy and singing the rebel songs that got them the name of the 'Fighting Irish'. Strange he had never heard any of those songs until he got to France. He could hear Kettle roaring 'A Nation Once Again' and see Emmet Dalton's deprecating smile. For there wasn't a lot of the mad Irishman in Dalton, not until the action began anyway.

Larry's enchanted face looked upwards into his. Allowing there had been a couple of years between them when they ran wild on the hill together war most bloody had catapulted Rory into a hard learned manhood while the other had been just cruising along under his mother's care and domination. Just look at him now. Nearly six feet tall and still in short trousers which hugged his reddened thighs and shamelessly delineated the man-size weapon underneath. Someone should have told him about it, but the lad himself seemed to be quite unaware of anything out of the ordinary. Rory took another look at the soft, childish face and thought, surprised that it had never occurred to him before, 'Larry is a natural'. The widow Mangan's boy was retarded and so probably were they all in that family. He himself felt uneasy looking into the wide, wondering eyes of a near idiot.

'We could set a few snares in the burrows' suggested Larry. 'Or we could make a boat and float it down the river all the way to the bridge. I've got a tin and we could hammer it with a stone. Yer oul' cob'll be safe enough where she is.' And he reached up to help Rory dismount.

Disgusted with himself for the revulsion he felt Rory dug his heels into the cob's side and jogged away while Larry sank to the sodden ground and cried his misery aloud. Two years had he waited. Two years telling himself that everything would be all right again when Rory came home from the war. And now he didn't want to play.

'Hello there, Derry' said Constable Madigan.

'Hello yerself Misthur Madigan. Are they keeping' ya busy these days?

'Ah, divil a busy is in it' said the constable comfortably. 'Sure there's never no trouble in Gorteen, praise be to God. Meath and Dublin's getting to be no place to go for your holidays. But everything's nice and peaceful in Gorteen, all over Wickla for that matter. Is there something I can do for ya? The big red face beamed innocent goodwill on all humanity.

'No' answered Derry. 'I was just wondering' if y'd like to step inside an' take a drop, smoke a pipe at least. Sure nowan in Gorteen'll ever tell the Sergeant.'

'Now that's very kinda ya, Derry' said Constable Madigan. 'Days like this its a good thing to get out of the weather any chance y' get. But I've got a message to do for oul' Mrs Murley in this glen. A wee dropeen of medicine. Doctor Kavanagh says she has to start taking it right away. Blood pressure I think he said it was. But I'll take advantage of yer kind hospitality on the way back if you don't mind and thank ya for it' and he scooted his heavy regulation bike a few yards before swinging his leg across the bar with the practised ease of many years.

Derry watched the constable bending to the first rise in the road leading out the village. The he said aloud 'Don't mention it, ya bastard. Y'll be mower than welcome.'

This could be a test job for someone. Every man who volunteered for the IRA was required to do one killing before he could be fully accepted and allowed to take the chilling Oath which had come to the IRA from the United Irishmen and their origins in the Masonic Lodges of Ulster. Any man allowed in was in up to the neck. Having committed himself by taking a life there was no chance of a man backing out again and the ancient cancer of the informer was effectively excised. No one was ever allowed to resign from Collins' IRA.

The question was Who? It could not be Derry himself. He had done his test job at Jimmy Doyle's behest when he plugged oul' Major Simes in Bray an' him out walkin' his dogs in the moonlight. Then he had to plug the dogs as well when they came for him in defence of their master. At the time he hadn't liked it very much but now he could feel a sort of pride as he remembered the almost sexual ecstasy of his finger tightening on the trigger, slowly to make the pleasurable sensation last, and the sheer disbelief in the watery eyes of a man who thought he was safe because his family had lived at Old Court for hundreds of years.

If only he knew it, that was his crime.

FOUR

The fickle sunshine filtered through the lace curtains and picked out what was left of colour in the Turkish carpet. Breakfast was over and here they were each privately considering what had to be done for the day or what they wished to do for the day. Lavinia sat straightforward as usual by the stone fireplace looking into the pulsing smoke as if there might be a message in it while Constance sat at a table below the window and wondered what she could put in a letter home that she had not already told them before.

In a faded easy-chair Rory enjoyed the first pipe of the day while he scanned the newspapers which had arrived too late last night to be read properly. What he saw there he did not very much like for it seemed to him that the whole country must have gone mad. Policeman shot - Madigan down in the village had not been the only one: they seemed to be shooting policemen all over the place - and for what reason none could even guess. For these were very ordinary men who just happened to have found a safe job in the Royal Irish Constabulary, as Irish as any others in the land and Catholics to a main. It just did not make sense.

As he stirred in the chair the golden retriever sprawled across his feet moved sulkily and found another comfortable position as Rory patted its head and murmured 'Easy, Sheila. Easy, old girl' and got a lick in return.

Sheila had been Andrew's dog, given to him by old Admiral Barry when the never-to-be-forgotten Mulligan had been killed by one of the very rare motorcars ever to come through Gorteen. A man of delicate sensibilities was the Admiral. Where another man might have said 'I've brought you a new dog, Andrew' the old chap had explained that he would be grateful if they would give it a home since his own bitches resented the new dog and might well attack it. Old bore and all that he undoubtedly was Rory had always loved the Admiral for that. As for Andrew, he idolised the animal as much as Sheila idolised him, never ever see one without the other until Andrew went off to war and then the bitch was disconsolate and off her food until, fully two days before the War Office telegram had come, she knew her master was no more and wailed her sorrow into the night, and after that she wailed or barked no more.

Rory remembered there had been some talk of having her put down and he himself arguing that no dog should ever be put down at the age of five if it was not vicious and finally it had been decided to everyone's relief that they would just wait and see how matters turned out. Then when Rory returned from war Sheila took to him as if it was her own master come back again. Though Lavinia insisted it was merely because he was a man and that gun dogs are mens' dogs by nature. Now it was unusual for Rory to leave the house unaccompanied by the golden siren unless he deceived the poor creature by letting himself out through he conservatory which had been falling down for so long that no one bothered about it any more. Such times as he had a need for thinking, a need which grew more and more frequent as he studied through newspapers the chaotic politics of the times to try to discover a point of view of his own. The old Rory would not have bothered. But the old Rory had not heard men screaming as they twisted in their last agonies on rusted barged wire.

'Has anyone heard anything of the Admiral?' he asked the room. Something had put the name into his mind and there had been far too much silence recently.

His mother said mildly that she expected he was what he would have called 'confined to quarters' by his rheumatism. 'He usually gets it badly this time of year' she finished. 'And it doesn't get better as he grows older. Living alone as he does I think he should sell up and find a little place somewhere in England. I'm sure he would be much happier there.'

Rory thought not but did not mention that. Instead, he said 'I think I'll ride across to Iveraun and pay him a visit one of these days.'

His mother smiled. 'Oh would you? He would be very pleased. You could take him some of your newspapers. he would be very glad of that' which was exactly what Rory wanted to do. Tedious and opinionated as he was the Admiral had lived for eighty years and was a man whose opinion should be treated with respect. Not that he expected the Admiral to share his own interest in Home Rule, but they were both of ascendancy stock and it might be useful to hear what he thought of current developments.

Spasmodic and erratic as it was Rory could mot make himself believe that the horrors he read about daily could be as bad as they were reported to be. Of course, he thought, any killing is bad. But there could be good reasons for killing. It all depended on one's point of view. It hardly seemed likely that men were being killed for no reason at all even if the reasons were not particularly good ones. From the vantage point of his years the Admiral would know a lot more than he could ever hope to on the subject. 'I think maybe I'll ride across to Iveraun today' he said tentatively. 'Maybe the Admiral will give me lunch but I'd like to see him anyway. If you wish me to take anything for him I expect to be off in half an hour.'

Constance looked up from her writing. 'Would you like me to come with you?' she asked. 'I'd rather like to see him myself and it is a lovely day for a ride.'

As she started to put her writing things away Rory said, more abruptly than he intended 'If you don't mind, Constance, I'd like to see the Admiral alone. There are things I want to talk to him about. Later on we can ride across to Dunooley if you like, if the weather holds. It so seldom does in this place.'

The two women exchanged glances silently. When Rory left the room to collect his hat and riding cape Constance said anxiously 'I do hope he is not going to do anything foolish, Lavinia. I though he would be over it by this but last night he was ransacking the library for books on Irish history and he was almost rude when I asked him what he was looking for. And I know he posted a list to Easons last thing before going to bed. It seems a strange interest to me. What on earth does he want books on <u>Irish</u> history for?'

Lavinia twisted her wheelchair around to face her daughter-in-law. 'Maybe he is going to write a family history' she suggested. 'His father always intended to but somehow it never got started. Rory is very proud of being an Aylmer. An Aylmer came out for Elizabeth at Templecroney and was dubbed Knight of the Lee for it. Unfortunately it was never promulgated. I expect that will be it. Rory will be seeing what the Admiral can tell him of the family history. They used to be such good friends. The Admiral and Rory's father I mean. Yes, that will be it. Rory will be trying to find out what the Admiral can tell him about the family. Rory is the last of the line' she ended wistfully. 'Unless he marries, of course. But there doesn't seem to be much chance of that as things stand. I had rather hoped he would be going to see the Rector. After all, it isn't as if you and Andrew had actually consummated your marriage.'

Constance sat bolt upright. 'The cunning old vixen!' she thought and wondered if Andrew had confided everything to his mother or if it was just a shrewdly aimed shot in the dark.

For the life of her she could not guess whether what had happened at Mulranny counted as a consummation or not in the eyes of the church. But it was true that she and Rory had become very close friends, closer perhaps than they should be although he gave no sign of being aware of it. That she did not love him she could not in all honesty say. But she would not like it very much if he upped and married someone else, and as far as she was concerned their present amiable relationship could continue forever.

But the old lady had set her thinking about something which up to now had only been a vague idea floating at the back of her mind. If it so happened - and she had no reason for imagining it ever would - that Rory in that casual way of his proposed marriage to her would she accept or not? Probably, yes. For one thing she knew Rory much better than she had known Andrew before their wedding and she rather thought Rory would have fewer inhibitions than his elder brother and was more mature. Even if there was little of romance in such a union it would nevertheless be a suitable one, especially with so many eligible young men killed in the war and the restricted nature of Anglo-Irish society. Ascendancy was a word she did not use even to herself for that had been coined by the natives to distinguish between themselves and the ruling class, for the Irish can find the wounding word quicker and more accurately than any other race. The native Irish, that is. Those secret people who can be arrogant in subservience and hide an insult in a compliment.

If Lavinia was right - and it was just barely possible that she was - it would go some way to explaining Rory's occasional moodiness and his sudden inclinations to take long walks and return tight-lipped and unwilling to say where he had been.

Suddenly the room was flooded with sunlight and the birds were singing in every tree. And life had begun again. From the distance the massive bulk of Iveraun House, many windowed and built of ageless Wicklow granite, looked imposing. Close up the signs of neglect and decay were easily seen in the weed-grown drive and nature's topiary, windows as dull and lifeless as the eyes of a blind man. Though it might well stand for another two hundred years the hand of death was already upon it.

When Rory tugged the paint-encrusted bell-pull he heard a faint sound somewhere within, so it was working all right. He waited, thinking that he had never known the door or Iveraun House to be locked before, until it was opened to him by a dumpy little woman in a rusty black dress with tendrils of grey hair escaping from beneath a soiled mob cap which was probably the cause of the delay. Anyone calling at the front door was likely to be 'quality' and Letty Holland not only knew her place but also liked keeping it.

The old face relaxed when she saw the caller. 'Well if it isn't Master Rory' she cried. 'Come in, come in, come in. Sure it does me heart good to see you so it does. And how's everyone at Gorteen?'

It was a ritual question and Rory gave the ritual answer. Then he said 'I've come to see the Admiral. They tell me he isn't feeling all that grand.'

Again the old face beamed on him. 'Sure I didn't think it was oul' Letty Holland you'd come to see, though I mind well the times yourself and Master Andrew would walk all the way here for a tea of honey cakes. If its himself you want to see I'm afraid you'll have to be climbing the stairs for he hasn't been down for weeks with the rheumatism. Not that I don't get a touch of it meself on and off. But we mustn't complain, must we? Things could always be worse' and she led the way, her dumpy body lurching from side to side with each step, up a wide staircase covered by faded carpet secured by greening brass rails.

Rory had not been up these stairs since his short pants days. Now he could not help noticing the general air of decay, the dullness of the paintwork and the despair of bygone Barrys peering reproachfully from ornate frames which once showed bravely gilt to the breeched gallants and damasked ladies as they ascended these same stairs on the way to the great reception room which ran the length of the house.

Another flight and then Letty stopped before a mahogany double door. 'I'd best warn him first' she said. 'The Admiral doesn't like to be caught and him not looking his best.' With that she knocked loudly on the door and called 'You'll never guess whose come to see you, Admiral. Young Master Rory from Gorteen no less. Will I show him in now, sir? At don't be bothering yerself about that, you're nate enough. Go you inside, Master Rory' and then there was the Admiral, fully dressed but with a rug about his knees, struggling to rise from a chair before a roaring wood fire. 'Welcome, welcome, welcome, Rory' he said, his old eyes glistening with what might have been a tear if he was the sort of man to allow himself that luxury. 'It's good of you to come all this way to see an old invalid.'

Rory did not remember ever having been in this room before. Vast, it was, with an ornately moulded ceiling now ingrained with dust. More pictures about the walls, one decidedly a Romney but the rest all battles of another age with someone on horseback directing things in the foreground. They, he thought, would have been the Barrys of the time and wondered how it happened that the last of a distinguished military line

60

should have chosen to take to the sea. His eye registered an enormous Chinese dragon in blue porcelain and a mahogany desk before the window with a silver writing set and a spotted blotter bearing the Barry arms in faded gold leaf. Stuck incongruously in the dragon's mouth was a naval officer's sword with a lionshead hilt.

'Picked it up when I was on the China station' the Admiral remarked with a rasping chuckle. 'Carried it all the way home with me sword in its mouth and it's been there ever since. Tell me, how is your dear mother?'

Rory told him his dear mother was well and sent her warmest regards and that the same went for Constance. 'And how are you today, sir? I was sorry to hear you were not feeling all that grand so I thought I'd just ride over and see for myself. I brought you these papers, maybe would you like to look through them some time. It's really amazing how they can all print different reports about the same thing. I find it quite confusing.'

'Well, it's a confusing sort of a country' said the Admiral. 'You'll take a glass of whiskey with me I don't doubt. Mrs Holland, two glasses of whiskey for meself and Mister Aylmer. Wait. Better bring the decanter. No, no. It's all right. I know what I'm doing. It isn't often I get an excuse for disobeying the doctor so I'm going to disobey him now. You'll stay to lunch, Rory? Except that we call it dinner now. I always have my dinner at one o'clock nowadays so Mrs Holland can get home for her husband's tea. Poor man has the sciatica something cruel and she doesn't like leaving him alone in the evenings. And sure I don't mind what time I eat as long as there's something on the table. I usually have a tray on me knee but Mrs Holland can put a bit of a cloth on the desk and we'll eat off that. Sorry I can't get down to the dining-room yet. Tell the truth I haven't used the dining-room or more than a year. Saw you looking around just now. It's the old study, my father's study you know. Much easier for Mrs Holland if I live in here until the oul' screws gets better.' Then it was that Rory noticed the single bed in one corner under a covering intended to disguise its purpose and felt sadness for the old man compelled to live in one room of this great mansion and to be utterly dependent on the goodwill of one aged servant.

Rory said 'I rather wanted your advice, sir' and the Admiral thought 'It will be about the widow' for he had seen this coming a long time ago and very suitable it would be too. Maybe the lad was worried about what those idiots in the church called consanguinity. He would tell him that all that nonsense only applied to royalty so they wouldn't go killing each other off the way they used to for the sake of a throne, it really had nothing to do with ordinary people. The Egyptians and the Chinese thought nothing of marrying their own sisters and anyway anything was better than getting married to a Papist like that lad of Grant's in Gleneageary.

'It was about Home Rule' Rory said. 'I rather wanted to know what you really thought of Home Rule. Do you think it could possibly work?'

Now the old eyes turned anxiously on him as if looking for a symptom of some dread disease. This was just as unhealthy as marrying a Papist. Cradling his whiskey in his hands he looked into the fire and said 'Not now. Nineteen-fourteen maybe. Then we had men like Powerscourt and Holmpatrick and dozens of others like them, big landowners. They were the natural rulers of this country. All that was needed was to legitimise them by Act of Parliament and everyone would have been happy.

'It's different now. All changed. In the old days land was power and the people liked it that way. They knew who they were dealing with, y'see, and they just wanted to get on with their lives without having to make decisions about things they didn't understand. Changed now. Nobody knows what they want. But whatever it is they don't want to work for it. Take over the estates and what would they do with them, them that couldn't cultivate a cabbage patch. I tell you, Rory, this is a terrible country, the most terrible country on God's earth. Could be the most beautiful but they won't let it' gazing sadly and hopelessly into the dancing flames.

'But' asked Rory. 'Surely you don't mean that we couldn't

govern ourselves?'

The old eyes came back to him and now they were arrows of light. 'Ourselves? What do you mean 'ourselves'? We are the Irish. We carved this country out of bogs and land that would never have seen a plough if we hadn't put our hand to it. Three hundred years we've been here. Is that the 'Ourselves' you mean or is 'Ourselves' the likes of renegades like Barton who resigned his commission in Nineteen-sixteen and went over to the Sinn Feiners?'

Rory braced himself to say 'That must have taken some courage.'

The Admiral bristled. 'That's' not the word I would have used. Barton is alive and well in Glendalough this day while others, your own brother Andrew among them, men of principle who would not renege on their given pledge, are lying dead all over France. Courage indeed!'

The lunch was not a success and Rory turned the horse's head homewards no wiser then he had been when he arrived at the crumbling mansion beside Lough Dan. Apparently age did not bring serenity but an unreasoning fear of the unfamiliar which no doubt kept them awake at night. It would be the same with his mother. People of their generation lived by simple and invariable rules seeing God as a little man in a yachting cap with a pointed beard and so steeped in loyalty to the Crown that they would not admit the right of others to their own opinions. And with the best will in the world they naturally resented younger people.

It had been troubling to hear the old chap, with God knows how many whiskeys and best part of a bottle of fine claret under his belt, suddenly expose all his prejudices against the native Irish. They were, he maintained, a lazy lot, unreliable and untruthful and treacherous to a man and many other things which Rory allowed to pass only because he was a guest under the Admiral's roof. There was no gainsaying that the great names spat out at him over the very stodgy pudding were Anglo-Irish names, men like Wilde and Wellington, Swift and Shaw and dozens of others who were taken for native Irish everywhere but in their country. General Lord French and Admiral Beatty were Anglo-Irish. Patrick Pearse, he supposed, might be considered by some to be an Anglo because of his Devonshire father. Plunkett certainly was, as was Emmet and Tone and Lord Edward Fitzgerald. But privilege was unknown in the slum home where James Connolly was reared and he, to Rory's mind, was probably the greatest Irishman ever allowed to live. All this he had learned through reading. The people within his own circle would not even discuss the subject and the ones who might know, the villagers and the estate hands and the shopkeepers of Gorteen would always lock their minds against him.

So very much depended on the accident of birth. Born the wrong side of the demesne wall he might have become one of his own labourers, and yet he could not wholly accept that. Talk filtered into the house through the servants of the man the Admiral despised as 'Valera' and of someone called Collins whose name was breathed with almost religious veneration. Would one of these be the man to give the lie to the Admiral's prejudices? It seemed unlikely for such men had lived in Ireland before and all had come to the same end as the heroic idiots who tried to hold a Dublin building against the forces of the greatest empire the world has ever known. Yet some vagrant impulse made him hope secretly that it might be so for the sake of the men left rotting on battlefields far away. Where the impulse came from he could not even guess. But it was there, had been there since he alone of all Ardnagoilte had mixed with their cottagers, played with their sons and eaten their potato cake as he listened to the dirges of a people who had much to be sorrowful about. A man trying to ride two horses at once he was in danger of falling off both.

He remembered the Admiral's last words as he was taking his leave with effusive thanks for a meal which he had not much enjoyed. Instinctively fearful of the rabble at his gate he had been positively agitated about the safety of Ardnagoilte. Had they any guns in the house? he asked and seemed disquieted when Rory laughingly told him No, that they were not a shooting family and that Andrew had given his father's Purdeys to Uncle Jack in Sligo as a memento. He did not explain that he would not shoot because it seemed unfair to shoot at anything which could not shoot back for he had never mentioned that to anyone, not even Andrew.

He turned into the beech-hung drive of home thinking that the Admiral was wrong about Robert Barton. It took exceptional courage to turn your back on your own class in Ireland and the doubted if he had that short of courage himself. What would the Admiral think? What would his mother think? What would Constance think?

As he rounded the bend before the house a gold comet shot from the porch barking her head off and falling over herself in excitement to welcome him. Behind the dog came a tall woman in black, slender as a birch and of an ethereal beauty which he now seemed to see for the first time. Suddenly he knew that what Constance might think was very important to him. But he gave no sign of it because that was not the Aylmer way.

Derry Keogh let himself out of the confessional and knelt before the altar pretending to say a penance for it never did any harm to be too careful. As he knelt on the hard kneeler with his hands covering his face before the tabernacle behind which he knew was the body and blood of Jesus Christ in the appearance of a white wafer disc he thought it was all right for O'Reilly to talk; even if Collins despised any company which did not strike at the enemy a raid on Rathdrum police station was out of the question. Ten men only he had and while he was ready to die for his country this moment if necessary he was not so sure about the others. And even if they were what could they do against a well armed force and them only with the rifle they took from Madigan and a little bit of a revolver with only ten rounds of ammunition which was all that Dublin had sent them.

'Get some!' was the priest's advice and it was easy for him to be talking. All he had to do was pass on messages and promise absolution in advance to every man while they would be lying out in the heather and peeing themselves in case the soldiers came while the bold O'Reilly would be eating his ham and eggs in the presbytery or soft-talking the adoring nuns in the convent across the road.

Derry would willingly have laid down his life for his country if he had had the chance, but when the gallant romantics rebelled in 1916 he was only a bit of a boy and knew nothing about the fighting in Dublin until it was all over. Now, while Dublin had ambushes of British troops as a daily occurrence, Wicklow still seemed to be asleep. Only last week at a place called Kilmichael in the County Cork units of the Irish Republican Army had smeared Black & Tan blood all over a country road and the entire nation was singing about it: even in Gorteen where they didn't even know exactly where the place was they sang songs about the Third Cork Brigade as if their own men were afraid to fight, which bit very deeply into his fragile pride.

'Get some!' said the priest as if prayers alone would put rifles into the hands of his men, as it novenas produced dynamite and rosaries the men to use it. Men were dying gloriously for the cause in Kildare and Tipperary, in Clare and Galway and even in the black North. But Wicklow's valour seemed to have ended with the O'Byrnes and the O'Tooles with too many people depending on the ascendancy landowners to see them clearly for the oppressors they were. Ten men, one rifle and one pistol, who could make a revolution from that? But Collins had no time for passive revolutionaries and cared little whether an attack succeeded or failed as long as it was made. And the word he had just heard under the cover of confession had come direct from Collins in Dublin and it was in Dublin they would be watching to see what class of men formed the Gorteen company and maybe thinking it high time they had a new commander. If that happened, if some Jackeen was sent to take over Derry Keogh's command, he would not be able to hold his head up in the village as long as he lived.

Jimmy Doyle was with Collins in Dublin for Wicklow was too tame for the man who outfought the Sherwood Foresters at the battle of Mount Street bridge. But his last advice had been 'Hit them hard and wherever you can find them!' And how could Derry do that when not even one Black & Tan had ever been seen in Gorteen and the military never came closer than the coast road five miles away. And even if they were all over the place what was he supposed to him them with? Collins would have said 'pitchforks' but you can't throw pitchforks at an enemy you never see and the worry of it all was making him a nervous wreck. This wasn't the way he saw himself when he took the Oath to fight for his country and write the name of Dermot Keogh into the history books. But - one rifle and one little pistol like a lady might carry and only ten men. How could anyone blast their way into history with that?

His head bowed low before the altar of God he prayed with all the fervour in him for a miracle of some sort, for men and arms and ammunition to attach the foe and cover the Wicklow hills with Saxon blood.

In the name of the Father and of the Son and of the Holy Ghost, Ay-men.

FIVE

'If it was upta me, Mister Rory', said Scoiles with the familiarity of long acquaintance, 'I'd get Sergeant Rooney to chase that young fella away and give him a good fright so I would. The Sergeant is not an easygoing' man like poor oul' Madigan, too easygoing' for his own good he was if ya ask me, an' he'll put the feara God in your Mangan forya can hardly take a step anywhere without falling' over him an' him all the time askin' when Master Rory, as he calls ya, will be comin' out as if the botha ya was still chisellers. I know the mistress has had enougha him peerin' in at the windas like he was a ghost an' he's getting' on the staff's nerves because ya never know where he's gointa crop up next. Let the Sergeant deal with him, Mister Rory. It'll be a kindness in the long run.'

Rory said he would think about it. He was truly sorry for young Mangan now he realised that the boy was forever chained in childhood and he wished there was some way to help him remembering that in the Freemasonry of youth only adults were peculiar. But he was most certainly not going out to play with the widow's son. Maybe he could find Larry some simple work about the place, something to help him grow into a man able to support himself in life. In young Larry Mangan he thought he could see something of the oxlike men he had led in battle. For their sake and for the sake of their shared childhood something would have to be found for the lad to do. But it would not be inside the house. His mother would never stand for that and even though he was himself master of the household he would never go against her wishes.

He would talk to Lavinia about Larry first chance he got but things were happening which could affect them all more seriously than the welfare of an idiot boy. For the Admiral had been wrong in at least one respect. Robert Barton was not walking about free in Glendalough: he was in an English gaol. And his cousin, the Erskine Childers who was somehow related to Constance, was sitting in the illegal parliament in Dublin they called the Dáil. So two of the ascendancy had been absorbed in the renascent nation and there might be others of whom he had not heard. He wondered who they might be and how it might be possible to contact them because more and more as time passed he became more and more convinced that his own destiny lay among the people beyond his gates, the ordinary people who were Ireland, including even poor Larry Mangan.

Lavinia would have none of it. 'I really do not know what has got into you, Rory' she said. 'Quite apart from the fact that I do not wish to have any more Mangans about the place the other servants would not like it. Servants have their own class system and it would be very offensive to expect them to associate with a half-wit like young Mangan as if they were little better. There is absolutely no question about it. 'But', she said charitably, 'I will do whatever I can to help his mother keep him properly. Really it would be a kindness to her if he could be found a place in one of those homes they have for people like that. And anyway they should be bothering that priest of theirs for it's really more his line of country, not that he will trouble too much for nearly every family in Gorteen has a simpleton in it. It's not in the least surprising, the way they breed.' She closed her lips tightly, resolved never to allow the matter to be mentioned in her hearing again. Home Rule indeed! As well give Home Rule to a barnyard.

Dermot Keogh's hatred of the ascendancy was generations old and it was absolute. As only a Celt can he hated the descendants of the settlers who had possessed themselves of Irish land. That they were mainly mild-mannered and courteous people served only to make the offence worse: they were in the wrong place. For a man should know when he has done wrong and here they were three hundred years on acting as if they had the right to rule a country which was never theirs to rule. Like his father and his grandfather and all the Keoghs who ever lived he cherished the ancient grievance as the sole reason for every misfortune which ever had beset them. That he paid rent for his ramshackle cottage and that he had hardly been educated at all were faults in the Ascendancy. And there was some justification for that belief although some men had by dint of ability and effort managed to claw their way to better lives in the towns and cities. Most of all he resented the Aylmers as the ever present representatives of a foreign domination. That they paid his wages had nothing to do with it.

Much of his discontent was frustration for he knew himself to be worthy of a better destiny than mere labouring. As a boy he had dreamed of becoming a hero like Billy Byrne of Ballymanus or the immortal Michael Dwyer who defied the redcoats from a flaming cottage in the Glen of Imaal and lived to enjoy his glory. Of such things had his boyhood dreams been made. Now a man, the ancestral voices called across the centuries commanding him to one more fight for the old cause.

In a desolate spot by Knocknagowna Captain Dermot Keogh paraded his company. And an odd collection of fighting men they were, ranging in age from white-moustached sixty to a mere lad of sixteen, all dressed in ordinary clothes with the addition of a belt or makeshift bandoleer to represent military equipment, not by any manner of means an impressive force. But these men wanted to be soldiers, they wanted to fight and if necessary die for a cause they understood but vaguely and they were following an age-old tradition. Odd looking and maybe even absurd there was still a strange sort of dignity about them for it is not the uniform or the weapon which makes the warrior.

As an officer should, Derry called them to a very ragged attention. According to the tattered British manual drilling was necessary to instil discipline and that habit of obedience which makes men stand and fight when all their instincts are for flight. 'Form fours!' he commanded and the men shuffled about uncertainly until one of them called 'Sure ya can't form fowers wid ten men, Derry.'

Derry corrected him sternly. 'Captain' he reminded the man and wondered what he should do. The manual did not say how many men there should be to begin with and he was in danger of losing face at his very first drill. Let this get out of hand and the story would be all over Gorteen in no time at all and they might even hear of it as far away as Wicklow town or Wexford.

An older man, slight and dragging one leg as he moved, said 'I know how it's done, Captain. Usedta have to do it on the Square at Portabella. Square-bashin' we called it. Every morning' we did it. First ya get the men inta two lines and ya number them off be the right. An' when the order to forrm fowers is given even numbers takes wan step backwards an' wan step ta the right, bringin' the left foot up smartly an' dressin' be the right and the yev get yer forrm fowers. If I' d a shillin' for every time I forrmed fowers at Portabella it's livin' on me own land I'd be today.'

There was a flaw somewhere. Four into ten did not go. But even as he thought that the old sweat explained 'A course ya can't make ten men forrm fowers properly speaking', ya hasta have what they call a blank file. Number tree stands fast an' the man coverin' him takes wan step backwards an' then ya have yer blank file nate as ya like. A course they has to be tould. The commandin' officer hasta say 'Number tree stand fast, the resta yez forrm fowers.' That' the way it's done.' And he waited for his commander's approbation.

Derry had all the instincts of the officer born. 'I was just comin' to that' he said irritably and the old sweat remembered too late that no private soldier should ever volunteer for anything and most of all that he should always let an officer make his own mistakes. 'Ya just didn't give me time to explain the rest. Ya never told me you was in the Engelish army, Grogan' he complained, wondering what they would think in Dublin of his having recruited one of the King's Irish, for anyone who had once worn the khaki was to be regarded with suspicion.

Grogan said cheerfully 'Sure I tought ya knew that, Derry. A course it wuz in the oul' Queen's time before you wuz born, durin' the South African War. But yer oul' father would have known, God rest an' bless his soul. A course we lived in Gortmore than.' Which explained everything for the

71

neighbouring villages were as foreign territory to each other.

This was no good at all, at all. The parade was getting away from him as each man turned to his neighbour and swapped a story of the rivalry between Gorteen and Gortmore as if they had all met after last Mass. No officer worthy of his rank could allow himself to be ignored in this manner. In the English army they shot men for less. Forcing himself Derry sternly called them all to attention again and said 'Well you can be the sergeant, Grogan, since ya think ya know so much about it but don't ferget who the officer is or it'll be the worse for you. You look after the rifle and make sure its in the best've order at all times or y'll have me to reckon with.' For the oul' rifle was getting to be a bit of a nuisance. Derry had never handled any weapon but a shotgun and all he knew about them was that you stuck a cartridge in one end, pointed the thing at what you wanted to hit and pulled the trigger. But a rifle was a different matter entirely. More complicated like.

'Yer hear that, men?' he asked rhetorically. 'From now on Grogan is the Sergeant an' yez takes yer orders from him if I'm not here. Now forrm fowers like I tould you an' we'll all march back to the Cross. Then we split up an' find our own ways back and never a word t' annywan about his night's work' knowing that every man was just bursting to get home and spread the news that he was in the Irish Republican Army. 'Now, on the command, forrm fowers..'

The newly promoted Sergeant whispered hoarsely. 'First ya gets them in two lines an' then ya numbers them off, Captain sorr.'

'I know that' Derry retorted, thinking that he might have been too hasty appointing this smartaleck to be the Sergeant. But he was the only one with any military experience. 'You're the Sergeant. Get them feel in two lines again an' numbered off...'

Grogan took over as if he was drilling proper soldiers on a barrack square and none objected. It felt good to be ordered about by someone who knew what he was doing. As first drills usually do the exercise came to an untidy end and the small column marched down the hill, soldiers every one of them.

Larry and Eileen lay side by side in their own secret place deep in the summerproud bracken behind the widow Mangan's cottage, silent because they had no need for speech. It was enough that they should be together for between these two a sibling affinity had existed from their earliest days. Often when the younger children had been tumbling over each other on the cabin floor the two eldest had escaped to this spot and shared secrets invented only to exclude the rest of the family. On this lovely June afternoon Eileen had hurried home after being released by oul' Mrs Comiskey and gone straight to the secret place knowing that Larry would be waiting for her there.

For all that they spoke but little, not even a greeting as Eileen wriggled through the tunnel of the bracken and stretched herself beside her brother so that their bodies touched, but only just. It was enough that they should be together and away from the outside world, Larry lost in his own childish imaginings and Eileen feeling her young body being filled by the sun filtering through the lacy canopy with beyond that the startling blue of a rainwashed sky and not a cloud in sight.

Today Eileen had the biggest secret to impart and although she had been sworn to secrecy the warmth within her and Larry's nearness forced her to speak. 'Larry' she said. 'I've learned a new game.'

Larry stirred slightly without opening his eyes because he had himself a secret which he would share with no one. Rory had spoken to him yesterday. Got off his horse to speak to him as if there had never been a war at all and everything was just as it had been except Rory hadn't the time to pick sloes or go fishing for collickers. But then he was the master or Ardnagoilte and had the whole place to see to and that must be a very big job. So Larry forgave him for all his neglect and was wondering now why they couldn't go horseriding together for they'd more than one horse in the stables of the big house and with horses they could ride right over Knocknagowna to Lough Dan or maybe into Kildare or even see what the sea looked like with all the boats and everything. And sure there couldn't be much to riding a horse when oul' fellas like Micky Martin rode horses every day of the week: all ya had ta do was get on their back and pull the reins and then it went wherever ya wanted to go. It was easy. It must be easy.

Eileen continued 'But if I tell ya yev got ta promise on the Blessed Vergen not ta tell a sowl because its secret an' if ya tell annywan God'll strike ya down with lightnin' so He will.'

Larry turned lazily on his side. Whatever it turned out to be this secret sounded like one worth hearing for no one took the name of the Blessed Virgin in vain. Worse than cursing that was.

'It's to do with this' she explained, placing his hand on her firm young breast and feeling the nipple berryhard against his palm while the eyes which were as her own regarded her dully.

'And with this' she added, letting her own hand fall on his bulging crotch with excitement mounting in her and her limbs quivering as they did in the hayloft the day before yesterday. Larry looked beyond her to where a caterpillar climbed a stalk of bracken and wondered if it would fall off when it reached the arching frond.

'Ya put this inta me an' then the secret starts' she panted, her legs spread apart and her buttocks making small jerky movements of their own accord until she lay quiescent, her mouth slackly open and her eyes looking at her brother as it she had never seen him before.

Larry kept his gaze fixed on the caterpillar tortuously nearing the bending frond, waiting to see it lost its grip and fall to the ground, wondering if the fall would kill it as he said, casually, 'I'd say that was some kind of a sin like yev got to tell the priest before ya can take Houly Communion.' And he watched intently as the creature reached the danger point and appeared to negotiate it successfully, wondering how such a little thing could do all that with its feet though some of the feet might be hands for all he knew.

'And how can it be a sin?' she demanded. 'Seamus says horses and dogs do it and who ever heard of a horse or a dog goin' ta hell? When then.'

'I still think it's some kind of a sin' persisted Larry, not that he was at all certain what sin was unless it was fecking apples of missing Mass on Sunday or holy day of obligation. He had a vague notion it might be one of them things the priest called 'the sins of the flesh' but no one had ever explained what that meant. He knew for certain that anything to do with his taypot was almost bound to be a mortal sin though nowan had ever said what else you could do but pee through it. Poor Eileen, he thought. She'll believe anything.

Poor Eileen scrambled to her feet and brushed off her dress. The troubling urge which had sent her running the half mile from Ardnagoilte had subsided to leave her with a warm sense of well-being and she was herself again. 'Got to go now, Lar' she said. 'Got the potadas ta scrub for the dinner. Oul' Comiskey'll flay me alive if I'm late so she will. Now don't forget, ya swore on the Blessed Vergen ya wouldn't tell a sowl about the secret. God'll strike ya dead if ya do.' Then she was off breasting the bracken as she slithered to the road below.

Larry watched her go dumbly. It was little he cared about her oul' secret as long as she remembered to bring him a slice of that cold pudding they did be having at the house if there was any left. Like a cake it was with what they called golden syrup right through it or a bit of one of them jam tarts like the English make. There was never enough to go round the whole family but he always had first pick because he was the man of the house and needed to build his strength up.

That Seamus Fogarty must be some class of an eejit. Sure everyone knew horses and dogs didn't go to hell. The only ones who went to hell were Prodestans and people who missed Mass.

'And you're really and truly sorry you did it?' asked the priest, speaking as a disembodied voice in the confessional gloom and thinking that the man ought to have had enough sense to see him at the Presbytery while Father Gilligan was out and that Julia Begley entertaining some of her friends in the kitchen and not bothering to answer the door to show her opinion of lowly creatures.

But the damage had been done. No sooner had he given old Mrs Mangan her usual penance of three Hail Marys and a Glory Be and slid the shutter open on this side than the words came pouring like a torrent through the grille as if the foolish man had not another moment to live.

'Yes, Father' said the penitent humbly with his eyes fixed on the blur which was God's representative on earth, whose one word could free his soul from sin and save him burning in hell for all eternity if he died this very might. For too long had he kept his crime to himself. Absolution he had to have if ever he was to get another night's rest.

'Well' said the priest tightly, for this was not a confession he would have chosen to hear. But the poor sinner trusted in him as they all did so he said 'Well if you're really and truly sorry I'll give you absolution and say a decade of the rosary for your penance.'

The shriven sinner muttered his thanks and hurriedly made the sign of the cross. Just as hurriedly he took his departure thinking that a whole decade of the rosary was a lot just for killing a peeler when everyone thought O'Reilly was on the side of the lads fighting to free their native land. Still an' all oul' Gilligan might have been harder on him so he might.

In the third section of the confessional Biddy Horrigan hastily assumed an expression of piety as the shutter slid open and the priest whispered 'In the name of the Father, and of the Son, and of the Holy Ghost, Amen' quite unaware that by some trick of acoustics every word of the preceding confession had been heard and the only thing Biddy did not know was who was making it although the man's voice was not unfamiliar to her.

'Bless me Father for I have sinned' she babbled. 'It is two weeks since my last confession. I cursed, Father, and I was inattentive at Mass and I had impure thoughts...'

The priest had heard it all too often before and he had long since ceased to be surprised that a woman nearing sixty should have been indulging in sexual fantasies, which probably only

76

meant that she had been reading one of those trashy magazines they sent across from England. But she had to be allowed to talk for that was really what she had come for. Although it was not all that many years since he was ordained at Maynooth it still surprised him a little that the whole parish seemed to sin uniformly so he could give the whole boiling of them absolution without leaving his bed as far as that went. But of course it was more than that. They wanted to confess. They wanted to be heard. And they wanted the priest to know they were not just nobodies who never had the chance to do a wrong thing in their lives. While the fat old woman made her well rehearsed confession he appeared to be listening, but he was in fact thinking he would have to have a word with Keogh. It wasn't good enough to send a murderer to confess without warning the priest in advance. It was simple mistakes like that which caused the greatest trouble in the long run.

Keogh's finely tuned insolence bothered Rory but he did not know what he could do about it. His mother would not have spoken to the man and Andrew would have dealt with him offhandedly and cared nothing what Keogh thought. But neither his mother nor Andrew had ever experienced the strange feeling of identity with the untrained men who had dared challenge the might of the world's most powerful empire for a freedom which could bring little benefit to them individually.

That was the sticking point. None of the misguided patriots of 1916 stood to gain anything by their rebellion and their lives to lose, so they must have been driven by something greater than he had ever known. And he wanted desperately to know what it was, if only to be able to dismiss it from his mind forever.

The newspapers were no help. Uniformly they condemned the men who now called themselves the Irish Republican Army. It did not seem possible that men like Keogh could be thugs and murderers and he was absolutely certain that no one would ever call Emmet Dalton a murderer unless he lied in his teeth.

Books were a little better. In the parcels which arrived from

Easons were books which told him more about himself than he could ever have guessed and much more than anyone of his own acquaintance admitted, for it was a peculiarity of the Anglo-Irish to believe that their history was the history of England and as far as they were concerned Ireland had no separate history of her own. At Wesley no one had ever taught him about Wolf Tone and the United Irishmen although they were almost all Ascendancy to a man. No mention had ever been made about the Penal Laws or the iniquitous Poyning's Law or the requirement placed on the old English Catholics to convert to the established church in order to hold their lands. And there was no one known to him who would be willing to discuss the subject even if they knew anything about it in the first place. Every day seemed to make it clearer that he lived in a wholly closed community which never dared question its own origins.

Times were changing. You could feel it in the air and sense it in the people down in the village. There was implicit insolence in their manner and if they sang in your hearing it would be one of those rebel songs like 'Kevin Barry' or 'Kelly from Killan', songs that Rory would have been happy to sing with them had they been willing to accept him.

When at wars end the Reverend Scrase-Greene thanked his god for the safe return of his own son he was unconscious of the blasphemy which placed the responsibility for the deaths of other men's' sons to the Deity's account for the Rector's god was a peculiarly personal god. It was enough for him that Simon had been spared in health to spend a short holiday under the parental roof. That Simon's most excellent wife Margaret was again in the happy condition of 'expecting' was simply another reason for thanking the God of Moses and George Vth for all his mercies and blessings. That other families might be less blessed was a fault to be imputed to them. As far as he himself was concerned the Almighty had behaved impeccably.

His dear wife Flavia could not have been happier with all her family around her and dear Margaret positively blooming in the sixth month of pregnancy which would surely end with the grand-daughter she so fervently desired. All Flavia wanted to make her happiness complete was a second bathroom and a kitchen stove which did not fill the lower part of the house with smoke, though this could be offset by insisting her cook, Mrs Bradley from Gortmore, kept the inner door closed and both windows open however cold the day might be. After all, Bradley was a country woman and should be used to it.

Now they sat, all four of them, enjoying the pleasant post-breakfast hour, the women chatting while the men smoked their pipes and opened their newspapers with that air about them which said more plainly than words that they did not wish to be disturbed. Maternity suited Margaret. It glowed from within her to make Flavia hope that this might not be the only grand-daughter she might have, for both of them were still young enough to add to their family if they so wished. Simon had grown exactly as she had wished, a sober man much like his father and like him in appearance also. Give Simon grey hair and a pair of reading spectacles and they could be alike as two bookends on either side of the huge log fire for the mornings were still cold and anyway they could indulge themselves for dear Margaret's sake. Mercifully the two boys were playing in the old nursery where they could do little more damage than they already had on previous visits.

With his feet propped on the brass fender the Rector scanned the 'Church Times' for news of old friends and, almost a mirror image of his father, the Reverend Simon put his long legs between his wife and the fire as he studied the 'Irish Times', vastly interested in the political situation which might well affect his own advancement with so many Anglicans taking themselves across the water for feat of the midnight knock or the blazing tar barrel at their door.

Since he did not himself farm he had no cattle to be maimed and he could not even begin to understand people who punished a landowner by cruelly injuring his innocent beasts but it was happening all over the country. In Tipperary, Kerry and Cork abominations were being done and there was fighting on the streets of Dublin. It seemed that only in Wicklow was there peace and tranquillity although he had been shocked to hear of the murder of Madigan, that RIC man, of whom no one in Gorteen had ever said a bad word. And the murderer would never be caught, that was well understood for all their pretence of shock and horror. He could not understand it. The gentle land he had left to serve his two kings had turned into a jungle of unimaginable beastliness: and for no apparent reason: it was the same land and the same people as it had ever been: but some evil was abroad.

For himself he had become sick of the place. In the deserts of Mespot Wicklow appeared a tantalising mirage of green coolness but now he had had enough of it and its everlasting dampness and the living of Rosgarman was not by any means what he had expected, an old and draughty house with oil lamps and a primitive wood stove for cooking and a woman who could not even toast bread for a cook. The church had been built for at least ten times the number of worshippers and the gardens of house and church alike were no more than wet wildernesses.

Soon there would be the matter of the boys' education for they could not possibly attend the local school and the nearest suitable schools were in Dublin all of forty miles away. Taking into account the present vicious political climate in Ireland it did seem wisest to consider a move to England or even to one of the colonies. For all their sakes it would be a move best not delayed too long. On that as on everything else Margaret and himself were agreed.

The problem was how to break it to his parents. That the Rector was content to end his days in Gorteen was both evident and understandable. But that would never do for himself or Margaret who knew that life did not have to be all damp sheets and church services. But when to break the news to his parents? When they arrived at the Rectory almost two weeks ago on their annual holiday it seemed only to be a matter of picking the right moment, but the old people had been so pleased that no moment seemed to be the right one. In a few days time

Jerry Shanhan would be taking them back to Rosgarman and then Margaret would be going to Dublin to have the baby and immediately after that it would be Advent and in no time at all they would be well into the New Year and still stuck in Wicklow if he did not get something moving soon. He decided he would tell his parents tomorrow. Not a pleasant prospect, but he could not decently put it off until they were actually leaving.

'I see that we're to have a new Lord Lieutenant' he told the room. 'Fitzallen. A Catholic. Perhaps that will pacify them.'

His father grunted a reply and went back to wondering if the Beamish in the obituaries could be the same Beamish he knew when he was at Trinity. Trouble was they never gave the chap's nickname so it was hard to know. The two women went on talking about babies.

Many problems the Mangan's might have but sleeping was not one of them, not even in the ramshackle two-room cottage they called 'the house' for they had no idea at all that they were a poor family. They had a roof over their heads, something to eat and each other for company. Poverty was another matter entirely and about the only thing they really feared was separation.

In the front room, entered directly from the tangle of weeds outside the door, was the common room used for meals and cooking on a fire which was never allowed to go out before the feast of the Holy Souls, 'redded' at night with its own ashes to smoulder the hours away until it was sacramentaly revived with a muttered prayer in the morning. On this holy fire all the family cooking was done, frying in a thick iron pan fourteen inches across and the essential stewing in a cast-iron pot hanging from a sootcaked chain within the chimney breast. On the heat-retaining ashes Mrs Mangan baked the crude loaves which her family would remember for many years after she was gone from them, every loaf baked with a prayer of thanksgiving. Beside this fire, in a collection of torn blankets topped by an old army greatcoat was Larry's bed which he shared with a dog of indeterminate breed which answered to as many names as there were children in the family. You would walk the length and breadth of Ireland to find a more contented animal than the dog which Larry called 'Spot' although there was not a spot on him.

Until about a year ago Larry had shared the inner room - the 'bedroom' - with his mother and sisters until the widow perceived that her son was verging on manhood and banished him for the hours of darkness, for which mercy he was truly grateful: apart from the comfort of the fire on cold nights he had a certain unease when his sisters skipped about shrieking in their shimmies and elastic-kneed knickers and was glad enough to be free of them, to observe the antics of the marauding rats and to sleep the deep sleep of those to whom even the concept of sin is unknown.

The bedroom proper was as austere as a monk's cell furnished with two medium sized beds in one of which the widow lay alongside her youngest with the feet of the next in age between them as sardines are packed in a tin. In the other bed the remaining girls, Eileen the wage earner and the twins, all looking startlingly alike with their bright red hair and freckled faces, slept head to toe in the greatest comfort under the protection of the Sacred Heart, Our Lady of Lourdes, Saint Patrick and the Infant of Prague in oleographs hung on the whitewashed wall above a red votive lamp with a china holy water font below it.

'Mammy! Mammy!' said little Bernadette as her mother urged them all into bed at the end of a hard day's work washing and scrubbing and mangling for the oul' melt up at the big house. 'Mammy, I haven't said me prayers yet..'

Nothing new about that. Nothing new about Bernadette trying to play on her mother's affections to steal another few minutes out of bed. 'Inta bed wid ya, acushla' said the widow comfortably. 'Sure wan warrm prayer is worth two could wans anny day. Inta bed wid ya me fine lady or its the weight've me hand y'll be feeling" although nothing on this earth would ever have caused her to chastise any of her precious brood. 'Are ya all right, Larry me son?' she called through the half open door.

Larry was more than all right. He was fast asleep by the redded fire and the oul' dog - Spot, Rags, Pincher, Patch, Rover, Val, whatever they liked to call him - was content to lie with his head between his forepaws lazily watching the antics of the night creatures for he had no intention of wearing himself out chasing rats. So everyone was all right. The widow blew against the palm of her hand above the smoking lamp and darkness descended upon the Mangan residence.

Children are lucky. The just close their eyes and go to sleep aisy as you like. But for them as has the care of them sleep does not always come easily thought the widow as she mumbled the prayers without which she would have been defenceless against the world. She thought over the small doings of the day, of how Eileen - God bless her! - had arrived home with a big paper bag filled with exotic luxuries from the Aylmer table. It was well ta be quality, thought the widow. Mate every day of the week an' all the chayse y' can ate when the likes of her and hers was lucky to have a big pot of potatoes with a couple of eggs broken into it to make a dinner for six. But Eileen wasn't going short, thank God. Filling out nicely she was. If only she could get Larry started at something. But there wasn't much in the way of work in Gorteen and somehow nowan seemed keen to give the lad a chance, why she could not think for he was a good boy and no trouble at all. Just wait until he saw the fine tweed suit she had hidden in the trunk under the bed for him. As fine a piece of Donegal tweed as she had ever seen in her whole life and hardly worn at all. Although she resented having to accept anything in the nature of charity from them at the big house she could not help being flattered when Herself offered her one of Rory's old suits that he'd grown out of and a pair of good brogues to go with it. The shoes were far too small for Larry but they could be bartered for a bigger pair at the waxey's. Then she would buy him a cap to go with the suit so he could go to the chapel fit to be seen with the best of them.

There was a lot to be grateful for.

SIX

Captain Keogh surveyed his company through unwavering eyes. His head was thrust aggressively forward and his hands clenched behind his back while they stood tensed for his next command. Not one of them dared call him 'Derry' now and from the original ten their number had grown to thirty ever since the word went round that this was no 'cod' army but a hard unit fit to be compared with the pikemen Gorteen sent to wage the same old glorious battle on Vinegar Hill in the '98 when for a very short time the Green had been raised above the Red and the slow moving Slaney had been stained with the blood of the foeman.

All of which went to prove that the Organiser had been right. 'Work them hard and give them orders' had been his advice. 'It makes them feel like soldiers. The ones who can't toe the line you're better without. I mind a unit in Kerry' he went on dreamily as if he was not inciting men to go out and get themselves killed. 'Had one man couldn't stand the discipline. So he resigned and went about shooting his mouth off until we had to close it for him. Been better to shoot him in the first place, to my mind. Or kneecap him or break both his arms instead of waiting until the damage was done. Still, you're the Captain and it's up to you how you keep order in your own company. My job is just to advise. You've got a hard job ahead of you but I think you can do it. Or if you'd rather the High Command (which was in fact two men, one of whom always did exactly what the other wished) will send a more experienced officer to relieve you. You could be posted to Wexford and Ross maybe, but not of course in your present rank.'

Derry reacted exactly as he had expected. There was great local honour in being known as the hard-nosed captain of the IRA while ridicule would drive a failed captain to emigrate even if he managed to get as far as the boat safely. And a failed captain was almost as bad as a spoiled priest. By the time the persuader left Dermot Keogh had almost forgotten he was still a farm labourer with his company pledged to donate part of each man's weekly wage so he could devote all his energies to the struggle. Later on General Headquarters (which was the same two mean wearing different hats) would probably arrange to pay him three pounds a week from central funds if he appeared to be worth it. But nothing could be promised. It was all up to him.

Three pounds a week would have made Derry Keogh the highest paid working man in the district, but that did not even enter into his reckoning. His ambition was to command the hardest fighting company of the Wicklow Brigade and to be recognised by General Headquarters the justification for his entire life. The money was not important.

So he drilled his men until they were ready to drop and the drills were held where and when the Captain decided with no dissent tolerated. Men arriving late on parade were tongue-lashed with abuse they would never have accepted from any employer and in at least one case a man rose from his sick bed for fear of the Captain and died of pleurisy in consequence. Not that it mattered: the dead man was deemed to have been killed on active service and his widow so honoured she was almost as pleased as if he had not died. One recusant alone had there been and he was in exile now and walking on crutches for the rest of his days.

Sergeant Grogan called the men to attention, saluted Derry and announced with a military briskness that the men were all present and ready for inspection. This was now serious business. Though there were still no uniforms or weapons the Gorteen company could never have been taken for anything other than soldiers.

Derry returned the salute with a negligence copied from the British and practised over and over again in the fly-spotted mirror above the mantelpiece.

'At ayse, men' he ordered as if he had been giving commands every day of his life. When they had all self-consciously shuffled their feet to show they were indeed standing at ease as proper soldiers should he continued. 'Now yez all know what our greatest problem is at this moment. We wanta hit the British hard but we haven't got the guns to do it with, not enough of them anyway. Thanks to GHQ (he spoke the initials with a particular relish for this was really being in the Army) we've got three rifles and two revolvers. But what we want is a gun for every man and as much ammunition as we can carry, and that's something we'll haveta take care of ourselves. So' he looked so sternly at them that some thought they had missed a command and came guiltily to attention again 'I have decided that we will carry out raids on enemy bases at Iveraun, Ardnagoilte and Saint Luke's for the purpose of obtaining firearms, to wit shotguns, and as much ammunition as we can lay our hands on. Places like that always have shotguns...'

'Not Ardnagoilte, Captain' interrupted one man. As Derry fixed him with a bleak commander's eye he went on to explain 'Not since the oul' fella was taken. Hasn't been a shotgun in the house for years.'

'Pity,' muttered Derry. There was no point in blaming the man although he should have let his officer know before this and them seeing each other practically every day of the week. 'Shotguns is very useful. Better nor rifles sometimes...'

'Plenty rifles Rathdrum' called a voice from the rere rank. Derry located it instantly. 'Speak when you're spoken to, Private Sharkey' he answered. 'Rathdrum comes later when every man in this company has a weapon of his own and the ammunition to go with it.' And when I've got a big black revolver strapped on my hip, he thought, like you see the British have. Every officer should have a proper revolver and what they called a Sam Browne belt across his chest to show he was the officer. Already he had the belt and Hennessy could knock him up a holster once he knew what size was wanted. There would be revolvers also at Rathdrum, he thought. Big, black service revolvers like the RIC. Maybe more than one. With an effort he recalled himself to his present duty.

'Well' he said. 'Orders is, Sections One an' Two for Iveraun an' do the best ya can but don't come back empty-handed. Sergeant Grogan an' Section Three comes with me to the Scrase-

Greenes.' To one man he said 'You do the best ya can at Ardnagoilte, no reason why the Aylmers should get off scot-free. After this night nowan'll be able to say Gorteen's afraid to fight.'

'What are we going' ta do to them, Captain?' asked one man fearfully. Gentle places breed gentle people and there is nowhere on this earth a spot more gentle than the pleasant county of Wicklow which hugs the sea between riotous Dublin and rebellious Wexford.

Afternoon tea was the nicest meal of the day, thought Rory, as he watched the Admiral hand his big breakfast cup to Constance who was presiding over the teapot of Irish silver mined at Dunalley and crafted by Nangle of Cork Street for the Earl of Bessborough.

It was a picture he knew he would carry in his mind long after the rotting men in boggy trenches were lost to memory, Constance, frailly beautiful in a mauve silk gown self-patterned with flowers and ivy leaves to indicate second mourning, the slender column of her neck rising from a bodice which hinted elegantly of the softness of the bosom concealed within. It bothered him a little that he had of late found himself imagining more of Constance than he could actually see and when she surprised him with a smile which was no more than a twitching of her lips it seemed that the whole room had discovered his secret although in fact the Admiral was asking Nellie if he might have another boiled egg and Lavinia seemed to be concentrating on spreading Gentleman's Relish on a slice of wholemeal bread while the Rector committed mayhem on the soda-bread for which Mrs Comiskey is justifiably famed. In the centre of the table marigolds laughed in a little brass jug and by the window chrysanthemums of bronze and yellow stood proud in a bowl of burnished copper. It was a picture to be cherished in the bad times which he was sure were coming. If only Lloyd George had kept his promise of Home Rule, he thought, and quite unconsciously repeated the thought aloud.

The Admiral glared at him, his cup poised halfway to his lips and rattling against the saucer with a bell-like sound because of his agitation. 'Home Rule?' he barked. 'As well give Home Rule to a tribe of monkeys!'

Rory clenched his fists lest he be tempted to assault an older man who had been his friend since before he was born. The Irish were not monkeys, he told himself fiercely. Then he realised that the Admiral did not mean us but them without knowing that them and us must be the same people or they were nothing. Constance looked anxiously from one to the other and Lavinia gazed stonily at her son as if he had never seen him before.

With a great effort Rory managed to control himself, passing his cup silently to Constance for a refill. There was nothing to be gained from antagonising people. Much better to keep a closely shut mouth instead of upsetting his mother and Constance. In a way he could understand the Admiral and even sympathise with him up to a point. But the Admiral misread his man and found glorious relief in venting all the pent-up indignation he suffered silently in the privacy of his own home.

'Traitors, every man Jack of them!' he spluttered, and he was going to have his say even if it meant being forbidden Ardnagoilte forevermore. 'Murdering and burning. If the Germans had won the war they would have known how to treat the scum. Keep them down. Rub their noses in it. Take reprisals three to one for every loyal Irishman they murdered. Kaiser Bill would have known how to treat them, had them singing 'Deutschland Uber Alles' morning, noon and night. We're too soft, that's the trouble, too soft by half. Big mistake. More always wants more in this cursed country. God knows I've no time for the Germans but they would have known how to deal with this rabble. The iron hand. That's the only thing they understand. Treat them decent and they despise you for it.

Before Mister Lloyd George is finished they'll have us all going to Mass and singing 'God Bless The Pope' if they haven't drowned us all in the nearest bog. If I was a younger man I'd be with the Auxiliaries today and that's where you should be if you're a man at all.' The old chap looked from one to another with staring eyes and lips quivering as if he was about to cry. Constance looked from him in pain and Lavinia's mouth was a dead straight line across her wrinkled face.

'I think maybe we had better not discuss this again' said Rory slowly with his own eyes fixed on the marigolds as if they were of absorbing interest. 'Not all of us feel the same but we are all entitled to hold our own opinions.'

'We are not!' shouted the Admiral, gripping the chair arm as if he was trying to rise. 'We have two loyalties. To God and the King. There is no question of an opinion about it. It is a matter of duty as you should well know.'

The Rector feared the worst and wished he could think of something to change the subject. This had the making of a scene which would be disgraceful in another person's house. But Rory had always been a well-mannered lad, he would never be rude to an older man. All the same it was a bit rich for a man who had never been in battle to impute disloyalty to one who had faced enemy fire for his sovereign. To hide his embarrassment he helped himself to another slice of soda bread and spread it liberally with wholefruit strawberry jam.

He need not have worried. Rory knew the Admiral was only spitting out the poison of years, and he himself would have no part in allowing a disagreement to become a quarrel. But 'I don't think it's simply a question of loyalty, sir' he said, more stiffly than he intended to but he was trying hard not to overreact to what he privately thought was a monstrous suggestion. 'I simply feel that perhaps we isolate ourselves too much, do not involve ourselves in local matters as much as perhaps we should. Maybe we should try to know our countrymen better' - he groped for the word - 'integrate more with them. It seems such a shame that we should be living parallel lives in what is after all a small country without having any contact between us. It will have to happen one day.'

'I doubt that, Rory' said the Rector mildly. 'That was what did for the Normans. They integrated themselves out of existence if what you really mean by integration is intermarriage and that sort of thing. It just doesn't work. The exclusivity which you appear to deplore so much is the only reason why we are still here. With integration they would simply have swamped us as they did the Normans. And they wouldn't give us a thank-you for it, you know. They like being as they are. Last thing they want is a lot of hybrids of indeterminate origins so that no one knows any more what's what or who's who. Best left alone in my opinion.'

Greatly daring, Rory said 'Surely what I'm talking about is simple Christianity? Christ did not mind living among what you call a lot of hybrids.'

'Rory!' Lavinia was shocked beyond measure by this reference which she felt was in some way blasphemous while Constance added unneeded water to the teapot and fussed with plates and the cake stand, fearful that all this could only to more ill feeling. In her most secret heart she was sure Rory was wrong although nothing would ever have made her say so.

The Rector arranged the crumbs on his plate into a little mound, resolved not to be drawn any further into a discussion which for him had taken a very distasteful turn. But the Admiral could not resist saying 'We all know what they did to Christ ...'

'Admiral' said Lavinia sternly. 'I will not have Our Saviour's name used in silly arguments in my house. If it is still my house, I mean' with a look of almost contemptuous reproach towards her son whose house it really was.

'Of course, mother' said Rory in a placatory tone, surprised to think that Christ also lived in an occupied country without advocating rebellion, so maybe the Rector's attitude was correct theologically. But theology was one thing and facts were another and at times one seemed to cancel the other out. 'First rule of the mess, Admiral, as you well remember, sir, is no discussion of religion or ladies names. So if you don't mind we will leave the matter where it is and never refer to it again. Tell me, how are the crops at Iveraun? We are finding quite a lot of mildew in the barley and for the life of me I can't think what to do about it. Neither does Nolan, and he is very sound on these things, thinks barley will never do well on our land. I would be grateful for the benefit of your opinion.

So the argument petered out by common consent. But when both Admiral and Rector had taken their leave with that additional cordiality which comes from a disagreement between friends Lavinia said 'I do think you should have apologised to the Admiral. He is an old man and he was a guest in our house.'

'Of course I should' Rory assured her. 'But I should not have meant it. I would have been telling a lie for the sake of convention and I'm sure you would not wish me to do that. Please try to understand that I have not the slightest sympathy with people who go round shooting other people and burning their houses. But I think I understand why they do it even if they do not wholly understand themselves.'

Lavinia gave him a long, sad look as she motioned Constance to help her from the room. Rory thought Why did I say that? Why should I hurt my mother and my oldest friends for the sake of a people I know nothing about, people who have no good feelings for me? He could think of no rational answer except that he felt something - what he did not quite know and perhaps never would - for the people who lived beyond the walls of the big house; and there was a sense of doom upon him.

Taking the short cut through the park to the Rectory Mr Scrase-Greene thought the real trouble is that the Romans never came here to invigorate them and dispel their antediluvian thinking. That the Greeks had been here he was quite certain. For surely the Goidelec ancestors of the Gaels - Mileadh, Heremon and Ir whom tradition said came from the north of Spain in the grey dawn of prehistory - would have been Greeks. For it was known that the Hellenes colonised as far as Naples and Marseilles and that as the Keltoi they spread into northern Spain, restless people that they were, and surely from there to Ir-land. There was much of them to be seen in the nature of the Irish race with their dark legends and sombre moods like Greeks exiled from the all-forgiving sun. There were so many similarities between the two races. Theseus and Finn MacCumhail might have had a common ancestor and Greek Helen and Irish Devorgilla both devastated their countries for an adulterous passion. Was not the cattle raid of Cooley almost the same legend as the Bull from the Sea adapted to the idiom of the Irish peasantry, the secret race whose dirges distantly echoed the plaintive melodies of Greece. And did not the two languages bear striking resemblances in the structure of their sentences and nostalgia for ages long past yet somehow still present. In the Rector's mind there was little doubt that the native Irish were in fact Greeks in the wrong place. But there he would have to leave it because he did not know any person of Gaelic ancestry to put the proposition to, and that was an ever-present source of regret. He talked to them, of course. And they talked to him. But they never actually said anything and always behind their eyes was a thinly veiled contempt which made him feel ashamed of his own forebears and a foreigner in his native land.

Through a gap in the trees he saw a figure crouched as if in hiding and he smiled ruefully to himself. One of the village boys. Had he been a Catholic priest the lad would have been bobbing before and raising his quiff in that enchanting way they had as a mark of respect. But a Protestant clergyman they would be afraid to meet in this gloomy wood in case they saw the cloven hoof.

Rory meant well. But he was wasting his time trying to build bridges between the native Irish and their most cherished grievance which excused them from making any effort to improve themselves, for the energetic ones had all gone overseas and what was left couldn't be bothered. Too many other men had tried to bridge that chasm and died of a broken heart because of it. Much better Rory forgot all about it and married that nice Constance instead of the two of them mooning like adolescents when everyone could see how much they cared for each other. If the Bishop would not give way on affinity then they should go abroad a while and have a civil marriage in England or France. No one would think the worse for them for that.

He had a distinct feeling he was being watched. Any by more than one person. And he was uneasy for all that he came this way most Thursday afternoons of the year. Then there was a cacophony of protest and a frenzy of wings as birds rose through the wood protesting shrilly to each other at the muted plop! which reminded the Rector of a pop-gun he had when he was a child. Perhaps a diseased branch had fallen from one of the strangulated elms. The sound was much the same. But the birds were used to that and they did not usually panic as they were doing now. Even as he thought that the birds somehow reassured each other and settled back in their home trees while the Rector continued on his way ...wondering.

How she had ever got hold of such a story Father Gilligan could not imagine. But Julia Begley was not a woman who listened to rumours so he had to pay some attention to what she said though he would have been happier if she had kept her information to herself.

Being the PP was no more than his just reward for a lifetime of devotion to the church, of saying 'Yes, Father' and 'No, Father' meekly during one curacy after another and being the one the housekeeper awakened when the Sacrament had to be carried to some poor soul facing his Maker at the end of a mountain track or a path through shaking quagmire on a winter night with sleet cutting your face and every stitch you wore soaked through with maybe not a fire to rest by at the end of the journey. And the terrible sense of guilt arriving too late when the troubled soul had already started on its last journey unshriven. Which was an awesome responsibility for any ordinary man to bear.

Time helped. In time a man could become resigned to his own limitations and hope that the God of mercy and compassion would not condemn any soul to hell because a young priest had been late getting out of bed or missed a turning or simply not moved fast enough. With the years Father Gilligan's concept of God might be altering imperceptibly. Against his own will he might be questioning things best left unquestioned. Which could lead a man into the awful sin of pride. And anyway the rules had to be obeyed to the letter: anything less could lead to anarchy.

But during the past ten years something had happened to the priesthood which he did not much like or understand. The men they were turning out of Maynooth these days were often self-assertive as no curate should ever be and maybe wanting just a little in proper respect for their superiors. It was a thing he could not begin to understand. The cornerstone of Christ's teaching was humility and charity above all else and these young buckos in their superfine cloth soutanes seemed to have little use for either. Which is why he had to gee himself up to assert his undeniable authority over that fella O'Reilly with the aid of a glass or two of Bushmills which is known as the favourite tipple of lions.

Mercifully the curate failed to appear for the evening meal so Father Gilligan was able to enjoy his pork chop in peace. 'Better leave a tray for Father O'Reilly' he told old Julia. 'I expect he'll be out on a call somewhere. A bit of cold on a tray and he can have it when he comes in' forestalling Julia Begley's objection before she voiced it. Let the man have his bit of food first, he thought. Then have it out with him, he thought, grateful for even a short reprieve.

Later when the temperamental bull who was his curate had eaten everything on the tray without even looking at it the old priest ventured 'And what kind of a night is it outside, Father?' O'Reilly said shortly 'Not bad' and seemed to think he had said enough on the subject.

But of course it could not be left at that. Allowing that the secrets of confession were sacred there was still the matter of church discipline and the Bishop was very strong on that, very strong about it he was indeed. Father Gilligan asked 'Will you take a glass with me?' and had the invitation rejected without thanks while the atmosphere in the parlour was palpably hostile.

'Out on a call, Father?' This time the curate barked something like a sardonic laugh and said 'Yes, Father. Out on a call.'

'Who would that be?' Father Gilligan wondered aloud, for he would know if any of his flock was at death's door and if he did not know then it was O'Reilly's duty to tell him. 'Not oul' Mrs Regan of the glens?'

'No one from Gorteen, Father' O'Reilly told him shortly. 'Man from Dublin, I think. Or maybe Liverpool. Emergency call out but it's all over now.' And by the set of his mouth that was all he was willing to tell. There was an undercurrent of defiance in his manner which troubled the old priest sorely; it was not to bring hurt or harm to others that any man took holy orders. 'Letter from the Bishop' he improvised. 'About the Eye Orr Ah. Very perturbed the Bishop is for fear of some of the younger clergy getting themselves too much involved. The Holy Father himself is very concerned about it the Bishop says, could lead to all sorts of trouble with the authorities...'

Father O'Reilly pushed his plate on one side and turned to face his Parish Priest. 'Well?' he demanded, as if he was a cardinal at the very least. 'Is that all you've got to say to me?'

Father Gilligan was lost for words. He had not expected this interview to be easy but he had not expected to be met with such arrogance as to give offence to Jesus Christ Himself. He wonder briefly if maybe the ancient Celtic church had all been pugnacious young men like O'Reilly who cared not a trawneen for any foreign Pope in faraway Rome. No wonder Palladius had to abandon his mission and leave it to the headcracking Patrick to bring Ireland into line with the mother church. He got a grip on himself. I am the Parish Priest, he thought, and this is my curate. He is bound to me by the most sacred of oaths to be obedient in all matters spiritual and temporal. All I have to do is assert my authority in the name of the Father and of the Son and of the Holy Ghost or I shall be able to call myself priest no more.

He said 'What I've got to say, Father, as your Parish Priest and as your superior is to remind you that Canon Law expressly forbids the priesthood from meddling in the likes of politics and that. The Holy Father himself has reminded us that it is our duty to be subject to temporal powers and to obey them in every way, for the kingdom of God is not made here on earth but ...'

The younger man's eyes blazed as he said contemptuously 'No man, no priest, no Bishop and no God is going to stand in Ireland's way this time. This time the enemy is going to be driven right into the sea, and if it takes priests to do that then priests it will be. For too long the church has been telling the people it's their sacred duty to uphold oppression in the land which was stolen from them, licking the dirty boots of a usurper in Dublin Castle and all for the sake of peace. Peace will not bring liberty, Father. Liberty will come only when they have to give it to us, when we are so strong that they dare not deny us our rights, when we're able to wrest it from them with our bare hands if necessary if we have to.'

The old priest slumped back in his chair, appalled by the blasphemy being uttered in his own house and by one of his own cloth. There was something about O'Reilly frightening in its ferocity. The man was so big, so powerful looking with his big red face almost black with anger and the steely blue eyes looking through the round spectacles like a warder at a Judas hole. This was the very worst thing ever to happen to Father Gilligan and he honestly did not know what to do about it. In the meantime O'Reilly towered above him as if to crush him by his very presence. 'That's blasphemy, Father' he said weakly. 'That's blasphemy and it's on your knees you should be this minute asking God's forgiveness. If word of this ever got to the Bishop ...'

'I wouldn't bank too much on the Bishop' said O'Reilly bleakly. 'It'll take more than any Bishop or even the Primate himself to stop what's starting in Ireland today. You're old, Father' he continued almost kindly. 'You can't help thinking twenty years back and I wouldn't blame you for that. But it's changed days and I for one wouldn't like to see you getting hurt over what you think is your duty. My best advice to you, Father, is to walk the other side of the road. If you can't see your way to helping us at least don't try to hinder us for we're going to win in the end. Walk the other side of the road, Father, and keep your eye on the wall.' Then, briskly, 'If that's all you have to say to me, Father, I'll be about my Master's business. I hear poor oul' Jimmy Gogarty is not all that grand so maybe I'll just look in on him and cheer him up a bit - if there isn't anything else you'd rather have me do.'

The old priest Peter Gilligan sat long after his curate had left him, looking deep in the heart of the fire and anguished in his own heart that things were no longer as they once had been. That a curate should dare defy his Parish Priest was bad enough, but that a priest of God should countenance the murder of his fellow men and that without judgement on himself and all he held dear. How could a God of kindness and mercy ever grant freedom to a country which held Him in contempt? And if he did, what use could they make of it, these men of violence?

All he himself could do was to pray. That he did into the small hours while the fire sank down to embers and died in ashes as he told his beads over and over again, asking God's forgiveness for Father O'Reilly and all others who thought like him. He was asleep in his chair with his beads still twined round his fingers when Julia Begley came in to draw the curtains next morning. And such was his appearance that at first she feared to shake him in case he should be dead even as she heard Father O'Reilly bawling a rebel song in his room at the top of the house. A fine way to prepare for Mass that was.

'Mammy-mammy-Mammy' cried young Nuala. 'Sing, 'Caw, caw, caw'.'

'Ah, sure I'm too tired, acushla' the widow Mangan said wearily. It was the sad truth. She was too tired and worn out with work even to sing a simple childish song to please her youngest and she in her shift ready for bed with the others egging her on. For it was a fact that Nuala could wheedle anything she liked from their mother and they would be the ones who put her up to it.

'Ah, Mammy' coaxed Nuala, her hair glinting bright red in the soft light of the oil lamp hanging on the wall.' Just wance.

Please!'

'All right then, alannah' yielded the widow who had lost this particular battle many times before and yet was pleased that her little brood should still want her to sing to them at bedtime. 'An' then it's ofta sleep for the lotta yez' she said as sternly as she could. When they chorused 'Yes, Mammy' like so many young birds in the nest her heart filled with a joy which more than repaid her for all the work and effort it took to keep them all together in health, for which blessing she thanked a god whom she could not even visualise. For it was a fine thing indeed to have a family and a better family than hers would not be found in a months walking north, south, east or west. Thanksbitta God!

Though the beds were nothing more than mounds of old rags and sacks they would sleep comfortable and happy as possibly they never would again for as long as they lived. Now they sat up and watched the ugly little woman who was their mother as she made several false starts and then pretended to forget the song. 'Caw, caw, caw, Mammy' sang Bernadette to give her a start and her mother rumbled in a strangely masculine voice 'Caw-caw-caw...'

'Said the oul' black crow' they chorused, laughing.

'Haw-hee-haw' said the widow.

'Said the donkey down below'

'Cheep-cheep-cheep...'

'Said the sparra on the wall - BUT 'and they all sang in unison 'The divil a note could Houligan's canary sing at all!' And then there were the usual arguments about who forgot what and who should sleep next the wall tonight which was in itself a sort of music to her ears.

'Now offta sleep the lotta yez' she ordered. 'If ya don't wanta feel the weight've me hand. Don't ferget to say yer prayers an' say wan for me special intention like good gerrls. Are ya all right out there, Larry?' When his voice came indistinctly through the half-closed door she said comfortably 'Good night, me son. God bless ya. Now don't ferget ta say yer prayers', for the only thing which made life liveable was the power of prayer

98

whether it was answered or not. Just as long as no unforeseen calamity came upon them the Father, Son and Holy Ghost, the Holy Mother of God and Saint Anne, the mother or the Mother of God, Saint Laurence O'Toole and the Little Fower and Saint Jude and all the others in the standing army of her heavenly advocates had done their duty by the Mangan family and she was well content.

The special intention? That was for Larry, of course. That the oul' melt up at the big house would find some sort of a place for him where he could learn something and earn a few shillings at the same time. Never mind the oul' melt being Prodestan. There was never a Prodestan born yet who could get the better of any Catholic saint if he was putting his mind to it.

SEVEN

One thing no Irish cottage ever went short of was soot. Inside the stone chimney-breast the stuff accumulated year by year unnoticed and disregarded as long as the fire would draw when the banked-up embers were refreshed with a handful of sgeachs gathered from the foot of the hedgerows to coax the heart of the fire to new life every morning. And if the fire would not draw a stone dropped down the chimney worked wonders or it might be set alight with burning newspapers as an annual ritual. However it was soot was never in short supply. All anyone had to do was to stick his arm up behind the mantel and collect a handful of the stuff.

So it was no problem at all for Captain Keogh to disguise his raiding party before they went into action although not all of them were really keen. 'Jaysus, Derry - I mane Captain sorr -' protested Jimmy Walsh, who normally pedalled his rounds on a massive bike as he delivered His Majesty's Mail to His Majesty's subjects in the general vicinity of Gorteen. 'It's like the Dixie Minstrels y'll be havin' us. We'll never get this stuff offa our faces at all at all.'

'You just do as yer tould, Private Walsh' said Derry, smearing his own face liberally. 'This is a very funny class've of people we're dealin' with now. If they can't say for sure about anythin' they won't lie about it. So if all they see is a black face they can think whatever they like but they won't swear to it. So. Every man. Plentya soot on his face an' remember not ta use names.' He peered outside the bothy, then said 'Off yez go. Hit the Saxon hard' as they filed into the night to strike their blow for freedom.

Simon Scrase-Greene first made sure the children were sleeping soundly in the room across the landing. Then he stole barefoot down the stairs wondering what the noise had been for it had sounded much as glass breaking somewhere below.

The Reverend Simon was a dutiful son. And he had been a dutiful soldier though he had fought his war with nothing more than a Bible and a cross of Irish bog oak to comfort men facing their last terrible ordeal hundreds of miles from home.

Every time the army chaplain Captain Scrase-Greene forced himself to follow in the footsteps of his Master he had gone in the secret terror known to most men in war. So he knew he was not a brave man. He also knew he could not stay in bed hoping for the best while all over Ireland wicked things were happening to people whose only crime was that their ancestors came from another land. This was his father's house and under his father's roof was his own precious family. And for his own he would willingly give his life if need be.

Just as he had risen from bed, without gown or slippers and with his bowels turning to water with fear, he crept quietly on to the landing, hearing the cry of an owl from the garden and feeling the polished linoleum cold to his feet. And listened, wanting to believe that he had imagined it all and that he could return to the dear warmth of the sleeping Margaret with an easy mind. All seemed to be well. Even the dogs seemed to be at rest. And that was not right. Then he thought he heard the sound of the front door latch being carefully drawn and then, beyond all possibility of doubt, the muted murmur of men's' voices, men who were as nervous as he was himself. Shamed by his nervousness he forced himself down the stairway and past the half landing overlooking the hall, a most unheroic figure in baggy pyjamas, eyes straining to see without his spectacles.

It was what he had feared many times. What had happened in many homes across the country was happening here in peaceful Gorteen. The blackfaced men could only be the IRA come to burn the house and everyone in it to the ground. Somehow he must rouse them and get them away to safety, that before all else. Shocked and irresolute he stood watching as a big man with the jet-black hair of a gipsy came from the study carrying one of the Rector's shotguns under his arm and brandishing another like a trophy.

It was over almost instantly. The man saw Simon just as Simon saw him and called a harsh command to another blackfaced man, standing just inside the front door. A shot shattered the quiet of the sleeping house and Simon Scrase-Greene's spirit sped to meet his God as the intruders scrambled through the doorway and into the garden beyond. Young Roger awoke with a cry just in time to see his father breathe his last where the lino ended and the gothic-patterned carpet began. Which is why the church of Saint Luke's in Gorteen stands deserted to this day and why Margaret Scrase-Greene is still a gibbering wreck in a nursing home on the Sussex Downs.

It was a very quiet funeral and sparsely attended for a family which had been well enough liked in the village. For there were not many in Gorteen willing to be seen openly expressing sympathy for 'one of them' although many wondered what the world could be coming to when such things happened to decent people. None more than the old priest Father Gilligan whose conscience urged him to show his face at the ceremony even as the Bishop suavely reminded him it was a mortal sin for any Catholic to attend any Protestant service. So he made amends by spending that morning on his knees before the altar, praying for the repose of the soul of young Simon Scrase-Greene and begging forgiveness for all Irishmen who committed such atrocities.

Not young Father O'Reilly. Sorry as he was for the people at Saint Luke's it was, he said, a misfortune of war just as much as the civilians killed in France and Belgium. And he too prayed for the Scrase-Greens, but rather half-heartedly as he habitually prayed for the heathen Africans and Chinese. As villages always do Gorteen kept its own council and its many mouths tightly shut. And, as usual, Lavinia Beresford-Aylmer came to the rescue by offering to have the funeral meats at Ardnagoilte.

'No. No trouble at all at Iveraun' said the Admiral to a man of whom he could remember nothing except that he was a relative of the Scrase-Greene's and came from the other side of Dublin. 'But if they ever come to me they'll get a hot reception, you can take my word on that, the murdering swine. Thanks' he accepted another glass of wine from Constance and continued

'Mind you, I thought we were in for it when I heard the lorry pull up. But it was only some soldiers looking for the military road through Glensmoleach. Lost they were. Hadn't the slightest idea which way they were heading. But the officer in charge was quite a nice young man. We had a jar or two and a bit of a talk and he was of the opinion that all this nonsense would be over in a matter of months. Auxiliary he was. Used to be a Lieutenant Colonel in the Seaforths but came down to captain to serve with the Auxiliaries. I tell you I'd be sorry for the IRA man who came across him on a dark night, or any other night for that matter.

'They tell me Flavia is taking it badly. Well, she would, wouldn't she? Only son. Served with Allenby in Mespot. Went through the war without a scratch and had to come home to Ireland to get himself murdered. I tell you it's a terrible country and it'll never be better until they've stood all the pro-German scum up against the wall and shot them the way they did in 'Sixteen. It's the only thing the Irish understand, the iron hand in the iron glove. Be soft with them and they just laugh behind your back. But I thought Barnaby put on a good show at the service. Must have been heartbreaking for him but he never gave a sign. That's one of the differences between us and them. They cry like babies about nothing at all. Without us this country would be nothing more than a big nursery filled with yowling babies. I blame Lloyd George. And this fellow Collins. Never hear of him getting involved in any shooting, do you? Gets others to do his dirty work while he lives like royalty in Dublin. Man I know in the Castle told me they could put their hand on him any day of the week but the higher-ups in London won't let them. No wonder we're getting all this burning and killing. If it was happening in England they'd soon declare martial Law and shoot every man Jack of them. And the sooner the better.'

'If I was a younger man' he told Rory, who had come to the rescue of the poor man at the wrong end of the Admiral's diatribe, 'I would go to Dublin tomorrow and volunteer for the Auxiliaries. Fine men. Ex-officers every one of them. Exactly

103

what we need to fight these murdering swine who dare to call themselves Irishmen. For what sort of Irishman is it who shoots an unarmed man before his own children? Or sets fire to the house of a man who has never done anyone any harm in his life? I knew young Simon when he was a lad running about with poor dear Andrew and a more amenable sort of boy you could not wish to meet. Maybe a bit too amenable for my taste, for I like a boy to show some spirit. But with the country as it is now we could do with a few more like him' and he nodded towards Rory who was slicing a hard-boiled egg from the salad on to a piece of bread and salt-and-peppering it to his liking.

Lavinia thought of all the times she told Rory not to do that before visitors and hoped he would not rise to the Admiral's challenge. It was all very well for him to talk but he had no son to lose and she had already lost one. And though the son she had left had not been her most loved she was gradually finding qualities in him which she had not suspected before. For his father's son he was exceptionally considerate and courteous and no one could honestly say that of Archie, amusing as he had been. If Rory wanted to go he would go whatever anyone said. That she knew because he became more and more like Andrew each day so it seemed possible at times it was his brother presiding at meals and making the house echo happily to the sound of his heavy footsteps clattering in the uncarpeted corridors.

Then she realised that Rory was wearing an old suit of Andrew's that the man he now was would never have fitted into the clothes he wore before he went away to the war. And that was somehow comforting as it was a comfort to see how close he and Constance had become. When all at the Rectory had had time to recover from their ordeal she would have a word with Scrase-Greene, informally of course, as if she were merely interested. She could just as easily drop a line to the Bishop but she did not wish to give her ladyship any material for gossip until the young couple had made their own wishes plain. Sometimes it seemed the Roman Catholics did these things better. From what had been called the 'Marconi Scandal' she gathered that they had some sort of court which decided these things and that rank and money usually helped. Which was very sensible of them, for otherwise what was the point of being anybody or having anything?

Rory smiled noncommittally at his very old friend and thought If only it could be as easy as that, to take one particular course and know one had done one's duty. But it was not. Nothing in Ireland ever is, he told himself ruefully. One side lets loose a crowd of armed thugs to terrorise decent people and the other retaliates by burning out other decent people so it hardly mattered which had acted first. In Dublin the authorities hanged a young medical student for being taken in possession of a loaded pistol. All correct and in accordance with the law, of course. But no Irish person had ever had hand, act or part in making the law and whatever idiots were responsible should have know they were playing into Collins' hands by giving him a martyr just when people were beginning to forget 1916. Someone at the top should have been wise enough to exercise clemency. For a whole nation cannot be terrorised into submission. Not forever. And least of all Ireland.

The other lot, the ones who called themselves the Irish Republican Army, were not a lot better. In some ways there were worse for they did not even put people on trial before shooting them and it was rumoured that the killings could sometimes be the result of old feuds: and that could be true for the Irish never forget a grievance however slight or unintentional it may have been. That woman they 'executed' in Cork, the poor old Mrs Lindsay they took from her home and gunned down on her own doorstep as an informer, no civilised race could possibly tolerate that and what would she have to inform about anyway? Most likely the poor woman's crime might only have been that she was a Protestant, in which case none of them were safe. Just as the Admiral said, it was becoming a terrible country to live in. Yet he could feel much that was good in it. But, all sentiment apart, what could they do? Neither Mother or Constance was the type to yield to threats and he did not think that he would either. But sooner or later a decision would have to be made. Give it another year at most and then sell up if things got no better. And if he could find a buyer.

To have to leave Ardnagoilte and settle in what he still thought of as a foreign land over the water was too bitter even to contemplate. Roundly he cursed Collins and Craig and all the rest of them for the havoc they had brought to a gentle land of easy going people. Most of all he cursed Lloyd George and Asquith and all the smug parliamentarians who could have averted the bloodshed by granting Ireland the Home Rule she was entitled to years ago. Redmond had been wrong to put his faith in an Englishman's word. They had all been wrong. But now it was too late. Like the flow of volcanic lava all the hatreds and enmities of many generations would sweep over the country and destroy its beauty forever.

'I haven't given it much thought yet, Admiral' he said politely while the old sea-dog told the room at large what he would do if only he was a young man again. The litanic response of the words 'iron hand' and 'up against the wall' set his teeth on edge until Constance came to tell him the Limericks were leaving and he went to see them off with the privileged Sheila pressing hard against his leg as if afraid that he too was leaving Ardnagoilte.

The raid had not been Derry's brainchild. The impetus for that came from a tubby little man who called himself Bernard Ferguson but who was in truth one Ernest Bernard O'Malley, scion of a well-to-do Unionist family which kept servants - nurse, maids, grooms, gardeners, all the necessary attendants of a prosperous middle-class household - in their substantial home in Castlebar in the county Mayo (God help us!). A man from a home which had never known want it had never occurred to him to question the English King's right to rule Ireland until the fires of Easter Week kindled the flame of nationalism in his own soul.

Now he had been sent by no less a person than Michael Collins himself to breathe the same divine fire into the hearts of the

106

timid and to encourage the hesitant to deeds such as they had not known was in them, a ginger-upper of troops in the nebulous rank of Organiser. And he was very good at his work.

When Michael Collins was told that he had an IRA company in a place he had never heard of he was not at all surprised. Anywhere in the country a group of men would band together and elect one of their number to be Captain and when by one means or another the news arrived in the office over the shoe shop in Mary Street an imprimatur would be given to legitimise the formation and its commanding officer. When more than a year after the Gorteen company had been formed no action against the enemy appeared to have been taken the Big Fellow judged it time to send his most persuasive emissary into the hills of Wicklow to preach the word. One thing which did please him was to find that the Gorteen company actually had a chaplain. Quite apart from reasons of morale (a priest could strengthen the troops by giving them Absolution in advance of an action for instance) having one of your side was always very useful. The man in the Roman collar could move wherever he wished unhindered and unsearched even into the prisons, which was a very great facility.

'Captain Keogh, is it?'

Derry was cutting out a stubborn blackthorn on the edge of the plantation, wondering why the old woman couldn't let it be and it not in anyone's way and it being well known that to cut the fairy bush brought bad luck to whoever did it, when the stranger came upon him. He looked up to see a roly-poly sort of a man in glasses and hung about with binoculars and map cases to beat the band and his approach had been absolutely silent.

'Keogh is my name' Derry said shortly, regarding the newcomer with suspicion. The 'Captain' he would not admit to although he was often as not addressed by that title in the village nowadays.

'My name is O'Malley and I come from Headquarters by the order of the Chief of Staff.' There was no mistaking the easy authority in the man as he reeled off names no outsider would ever have known so that Derry wondered he could have known so much and him never having set foot in the village before. So when the quiet eyes regarded him steadily and asked why the Gorteen company had not given a better account of itself he answered honestly that it was shortage of weapons and shortage of targets.

O'Malley said, as if he was musing to himself, 'But Wicklow is full of the Ascendancy, more than any other county in the country. The people who stole the land from you in the first place are still sitting there laughing at you. Take it back from them, or at least make sure they enjoy it no longer if you are a real Irishman.' When Derry explained about the one rifle and the little pistol O'Malley said unexpectedly 'Let me have a look at it.' When he had examined the trinket he said very solemnly 'Do you realise that pistol was used by Padraig Pearse in 'Sixteen? I don't know how you got hold of it but you should guard it with your life or, better still, use it to avenge Pearse and all the other good men martyred for the Cause.' It did not seem to be possible but that was what the man said, and what reason would he have to be telling lies about a thing like that? Derry wondered, handling the miniature firearm as if it was a relic of the True Cross and feeling its magic already working in him.

An idea seemed to occur to O'Malley, sitting on the ground on the edge of the wood and absently feeding tobacco into the bowl of a gnarled briar pipe in clear sight of Ardnagoilte. 'Who lives in that house?' he asked.

Derry told him it was the Aylmers.

'And where do they come from?' was the next question.

Derry scratched his head and said he did not know, that Aylmers had lived at Ardnagoilte for as long as anyone could remember.

'But they come from somewhere' O'Malley insisted. 'Aylmer isn't an Irish name, not native Irish. They'll be Protestant' he added as if not sure of the answer. When Derry said Yes, that the Aylmers were Church of Ireland O'Malley pulled on his pipe and said as a man who has been proved right 'Then they're not Irish, you can be sure of that. Irish is Catholic. Always has been since they hunted the priests in the hills for saying the Mass. Always will be' although he knew well that the whole movement for Irish freedom had been initiated by Irish Protestants. It was not his purpose to give history lessons. His purpose was to galvanize the company represented by this sullen fellow into an activity which would help create the impression of a nation-wide rising against the insolent crown. 'That could be your house' he remarked casually. 'this could be your land we're sitting on. Some Irish Catholic's land anyway, before the Saxons came and took it by force.'

The blue smoke eddied upwards between them and he saw with satisfaction that he had touched on a raw nerve. With patience this fellow could be made to fight. He was just a slowish sort of man but sometimes they turned out to be the best, they stuck to the job once they understood exactly what the job was. There was the makings of a success story in this. Another success story.

'Gorteen hasn't done much fighting' he remarked as if it was of no great importance to him. Again Derry told him they did not have either the opportunities of the weapons.

'There's guns in that house' said O'Malley, knocking his pipe out on a log and immediately refilling it from a bulging rubber pouch. 'Maybe five of six. Shotguns. The gentry are great ones for the shooting. They'll have shotguns at the very least.'

Relieved, Derry told him it was not so, that the Aylmers had never been known to go shooting since the oul' fella's day.

'There'll be guns just the same' said O'Malley. 'For them kind never get rid of anything. You need a man in that house.'

Smugly Derry said he had two men in the house and one of them his very best. 'I was goin' ta make him a sergeant' he added 'but he knew nothing about the rifle. None of us knows anythin' about the rifle.'

'That's what I'm here for' O'Malley told him jovially. 'When do you drill your men?' When he was told that the drills were not regular, that they assembled when it was convenient to them all, he tut-tutted like a school teacher and explained that would never do at all. 'They need to be made feel like soldiers' he explained. 'Regular drills gives them discipline and without discipline the finest army is like a hooley without the music.'

And where did they drill? was the next question and was it always in the same place? with more tut-tutting and a lot of talk about security. That had never occurred to Derry before but now that it was explained he could see the sense of it.

'The man of the house' asked O'Malley, nodding towards the squat bulk of Ardnagoilte almost hidden behind its thicket of rhododendrons and rampant azaleas. 'In the English army was he?' Derry said that he was, served in the war like his brother that was killed in 'Sixteen.

O'Malley sat upright. 'In Dublin?' he asked, for the men who served Britain in that incendiary year of rebellion would never be forgiven or even tolerated. When Derry explained that the elder Aylmer had lost his life in France on the Somme all O'Malley had to say was 'Well, I would keep a close eye on him if I was you' that kind never changed, they were the king's men all of their days and even more dangerous than the Black and Tans. 'They're known, you see. The people trust them. Perfect spies for Dublin Castle. Who is that oul' fella? he suddenly asked as a tattered figure appeared on a rise of the road beyond the boundary wall.

'Ah, that's oul' Shawneen' Derry explained. 'A man of the roads. Comes this was every two or three months. Dublin, Wicklow, Kildare (everyone knew old Shawneen's territory). Sure there's no harrum in the oul' chap so there isn't.'

O'Malley did not agree. 'I don't know. He has the look of an army man to me. Was he ever in the English army?'

Again Derry admitted he did not know, that no one really knew anything about oul' Shawneen at all.

O'Malley pursed his lips. 'Could be a spy' he said. 'There's a castle in Dublin and the headquarters of the occupation army is in Kildare. One oul' tramp covers three counties in a couple of months so they could cover the whole country with only ten men if they wanted to. Fella like that, ex English army I'd say, he's likely to be a spy. Best to play safe. Call the men together tonight. Then we can arrest him and give him a fair trial. After that we'll shoot him.'

And so they found Shawneen's body by the roadside with a card marked "TRAITORS AND SPIES BEWARE. IRA" pinned to his ragged jacket. Which made people who should have known better look knowing and confide in each other that they were not in the least surprised, that there had always been a bit too much of the gentleman about Shawneen for him to have been a real tramp. And because they had both given succour to the old travelling man both the widow Mangan and Biddy Horrigan found themselves coming under censure while O'Malley went on his way well satisfied with his day's work. Every man in the Gorteen company now knew how to handle a rifle and their Captain had no further excuse for being dilatory in his duty. And the killing of Shawneen in the middle of the demesne wood practically on the doorstep of Ardnagoilte bound them together in blood. Besides, the man could have been a spy.

Next night they set out again for Iveraun like a band of wandering Moors with the shotguns, the rifle and the nickelplated revolver and absolved in advance by Father O'Reilly. When the pinkhued mist in the valley became grey again Iveraun was a smouldering ruin with the master of the house lying in the great doorway with a bullet in his head and his naval sword clutched in his hand, the gilt knot at the hilt scorched black and the Admiral himself so badly burned as to be almost unrecognisable. Upstairs the T'ang dragon was discoloured but intact and the heavy frames which had housed portraits of his illustrious forebears now showed only tattered canvasses which might have been anything and over all hung a pall of smoke from the smouldering embers.

Rory was dazed with anger and unbelief when he heard of the raid on Iveraun, thinking bitterly that it took little courage to kill an old man who probably had not much time left anyway.

And he changed his secret opinion of Michael Collins whom he had grudgingly admired as probably the man best suited to lead his country to full nationhood. Now he saw the Big Fellow, as they all called him, as the very personification of evil incarnate, wondering what manner of man could order the killing of an eighty-year-old whose only fault was that he could not hold his tongue and whose only battle had been in defence of his own hearth.

Well, as the old clansmen used to say, we all follow our own piper even if he leads us down the wrong road. This man Collins had much to answer for. Of course it might be that the visit of the Auxiliaries to Iveraun had been noticed and misunderstood. It might have been thought they had called on the Admiral by arrangement and they were detested the length and breadth of Ireland for their brutality as much as their little brothers the Black and Tans. Neither Auxiliaries or Black and Tans had ever had any business in this part of Wicklow but their reputation was well known. He had himself once seen the Black and Tans in Dublin, roaring about in Crossley tenders and terrorising the population so that he felt shame that such ruffians should be allowed to wear the king's uniform.

'We'll bury him here in Gorteen' said Lavinia speaking her thoughts aloud. 'They may have driven him from his home but they'll not drive him from the place he was born in. They will be singing songs in the village tonight about how they drove the master of Iveraun from his land and not one of them man enough to face him without an armed gang to back him up.'

'But, mother...' protested Rory. He could not remember ever having seen his mother so angry before, she who had always schooled him never to show temper.

Lavinia ignored him. 'That's what they want, what they've wanted for the past hundred years, to drive us off our land so they can let it go to rack and ruin.' She continued dreamily 'When your father first brought me to Ardnagoilte the garden was a picture. You could go out any day and cut enough flowers to fill the house. But now if it wasn't for what we do ourselves there wouldn't be a flower to cut. Like a picture that garden was and now look at it. MacIver kept it in the best of order with only a boy to assist him. When he got too old we had two local men in but they couldn't do half his work between them.

'The Admiral had no relatives, you know. The last of his line and it will be a sorry day for Ireland when we've all gone. Not that they will admit it. Everything they make a mess of will be blamed on us long after we are all dead and forgotten. We'll get Wallers down from Dublin to make the arrangements, they always do things very nicely. And Gregory from Rathgar can conduct the service. You will find him in my address book. Saint Jude's I think it is but it's all in the book under G, if you wouldn't mind, Constance. Please write and ask him if he would be kind enough to help us bury an old friend of his father's from Trinity.

'They will never be satisfied until they have driven us all from our own homes but even if they burn Ardnagoilte over my head here I will stay to the very end, as your father would, and Andrew. I wonder if we should try to bury the Admiral with full military honours, whatever that may mean. Do you know what military honours are, Rory? But of course you do, you must have seen them many times in France.'

'It wasn't like that, mother' he said gently, remembering the unburied dead who were the detritus of every battle. 'Usually we just buried them and put a marker up to say who they were. (If we knew who they were, he added in the secrecy of his own mind). Military honours are a sort of peace time thing, bands and escort and a bugler sounding Last Post. I shouldn't think we'll be able to manage anything like that here.'

'Well never mind' she said briskly. 'We shall just have to do the best we can. Last of the Barry's, the Admiral. Been at Iveraun over two hundred years and now there are none left.' Quite inconsequentially she added 'Tell Mrs Mangan to send that boy of hers up here tomorrow. If he can keep the weeds down that will be something. We shall have to have everyone here after the funeral. We can't do any less for the Admiral. He was all alone, you see. No relatives of any sort. The last of his line, poor man. Well, I hope they're satisfied for they will never get such good treatment from one of their own. Yes. Wallers I think for the arrangements and Gregory for the service. We should have 'O Valiant Heart' I think. And 'Belmont'. The Admiral was always very fond of 'Belmont.' Or that thing he called the Navy hymn, 'Eternal Father' or something like that. The last of his line and then to be put to death like that.'

She faltered and stopped abruptly, gazing into space as if the was looking back down the years when gardens were always beautiful and girls wore white in summertime and all the men were brave and gallant, when the crown of England surmounting a harp was the unalterable emblem of Ireland under kings who were always wise and godfearing, when one's place in society was marked by presentation to the Viceroy in the Levee Chamber of Dublin Castle with every other man brave in scarlet and gold and the footmen in perukes and the last meet of the Gorteen hunt was always held on the gravelled driveway in front of this house and everyone not only knew their place but also liked it that way so there was never any hint of dissension and one could be friendly with the staff knowing that they would never take advantage of it. Dear, dead, happy days beyond recall. Never could Ireland know such happiness again.

She sat gripping the arms of her straightback chair as a kaleidoscope of her life in this house passed before her. Her bridal carriage pulled up the drive by hurrooing villagers and the big bear of a man who was her husband loudest of them all and ordering drink and food for everyone so that what should have been a dignified homecoming became a noisy and not very well behaved party on the lawn in the moonlight. The freshfaced young Rector Scrase-Greene had been there, not yet sure enough of himself to join in the festivities properly. And little Reggie Barry still far away from being an admiral in the thick of it, for he was Archie's closest fried here in Wicklow where they had been boys together. The birth of her firstborn and more celebrations because Ardnagoilte had an heir and

Archie so pleased the family name would continue that he took her to Dublin especially to choose the diamond sunburst brooch to show his gratitude. Then Andrew's little brother Rory and after that there were none of the large family they had planned because dear Archie died inexplicably and without any fuss in his bed after only a few days of illness.

When the telegram came to tell her Andrew had given his life for his King in that first botched advance on the Somme the sun had ceased to shine for Lavinia Aylmer and she had actively hated every man who returned safely from the war, even her own son Rory. But time can be kind and the sun will always shine again. Now it seemed she could see both Archie and Andrew emerging from Rory and with Constance at her side she had begun to feel a mother again and even dared to dream of grandchildren. Archie, Andrew and now poor, dear Reggie who had never harmed as much as a fly in his life. All gone. A big tear formed in the corner of her eye and fell unhindered upon her wrinkled cheek. Strange that it should have been the murder of bouncy little Reggie Barry which released the floodgates at last. But sometimes it happens that way and there is always a limit to stoicism. Little Reggie Barry. Bouncy little Reggie Barry. Little Reggie Barry on that cob of his riding wild-eyed ahead of the field. Reggie who had remained wifeless for a reason which she alone knew.

Her own fine eyes glistening Constance took the frail old woman in her arms, cushioning her head against her soft breast and murmuring little endearments as if to a child while Rory watched, his own eyes smarting with unshed tears which threatened to unman him instantly, touched to see how close the two women had become in the years which had slipped away like a long day since he came home from France. A stiff upper lip can weigh a ton. He dropped his hand on Sheila's head resting on his knee and felt the old dog quivering at his touch. Then he made a great business of filling and lighting his pipe. He realised that had Constance not been his brother's widow he could have loved her very much. But that too was part of the tragedy.

'I'll walk down and tell Nolan' he said. For the stiff upper lip was due to slip any moment now and he would prefer to be alone if that happened.

The Reverend Mr Gregory, freshfaced and aglow with enthusiasm for his calling, arrived riding a Triumph motorcycle combination, capped, mufflered and goggled for his ride over the mountains at speeds sometimes as great as 50mph. In the sidecar a young lad clutched the case containing the clerical vestments, a chinstrapped Boys' Brigade pillbox on his head and across his chest on a thick cord a glittering bronze bugle. 'Thought it might be a good idea' explained Mr Gregory, his blue eyes starting from a girlishly pale face under an unruly crop of bright red hair which could have come only from the far highlands of Scotland long ages ago. 'Ex serviceman and all that. Couldn't very well bury him without 'Last Post', could we?' and he looked anxiously from one to another to be told he had done the right thing.

Even at the best of times St Luke's church was a dismal place for the generation which had built it regarded churchgoing as a station on the way to the grave and tolerated nothing in the way of levity. The communion table was exactly as prescribed by convocation, two candle only where the Holy Romans would have had the place ablaze with light. The memorial tablets on the walls were so many statements of bald fact and no plaster saint would ever have dared show his Italianate face in this small enclave of the Establishment.

Now, since the Scrase-Greenes had fled the memory of their murdered son, it was even more depressing with tendrils of ivy reaching through the broken windows to lay claim to the whole inside of the church. Bird droppings were ignored by the tiny congregation, the family and staff from Ardnagoilte and an agitated Miss Etchingham pedalling like mad to coax a sound from the wheezy harmonium.

Clergymen are a resilient lot. They have to be. Mr Gregory sailed through the service in great style with a discourse which would have made the late lamented think he was at the wrong

116

funeral so many were the virtues attributed to him. Then with a ragged rendering of 'God Save The King' the pathetic little service ended and they bore the strangely light coffin the few yards from the church door to place it in the ground while the bugler set every rookery aflutter with the heartaching sound of the last salute given to every fighting man before retreating to the big house.

'You would think his own people would have come from Iveraun' Constance remarked as she offered a glass of wine to Lavinia, noticing how very distraught the old lady was and hoping the ordeal would not be too much for her composure.

'Be surprised at nothing from now on' was the grim reply. 'We are only getting what others have had to endure for years. Down in Cork good Irishmen have been taken from their beds and shot only because they were once in government service and some of them no more that counter jumpers. Iveraun stayed away because they did not dare come. This country is becoming a jungle inhabited by savages the likes of which have never been seen in Ireland before. From now on no one in Wicklow is safe, but while life is left in me I'll not be moved from my own land.'

Rory wondered if it could possibly be true that the workers of Iveraun, the men the Admiral used to consider his loyal friends, should have absented themselves from his funeral for fear of the consequences. It did not seem possible such things could be in this land where Protestant and Catholic had lived easily together for many, many years. But the plain fact was that someone from either Iveraun or Gorteen had killed the old man and put the torch to his house, so any evil thing could be true now however incredible it might once have seemed to be. Then he went to speed the clergyman on his way back to Dublin and stood for a long time in the porch watching the mist creep along the side of Knocknagowna while old Sheila pressed herself against his leg with all of a dog's boundless affection.

Rory filled and lit a pipe and stood listening to the small sounds of nature, wondering how it had all happened and how it could all be ended with decency before the country was pulled apart.

Drawing on his pipe and leaning against the creeper-hung pilaster he thought how difficult it was to really know which side was in the right, for there seemed to be very little difference between them. They both did the same things in the same way and for roughly the same unspeakable reasons. If the tales told about the Black and Tans were only half true then Britain had never yet sent a more unprincipled bunch of thugs to keep her peace in Ireland, although he was loath to believe that utterly for no Irishman has ever spoiled a good story by telling the simple truth.

He himself knew how war can brutalise the gentlest of men. And these men had seen war at its bloodiest, fighting, sleeping, eating and dying in knee-deep mud day after day and week after week with only the slimmest hope of survival to keep them going, covered with lice and seeing arrogant rats feeding on the bodies of their fallen comrades while they waited for the shellfall which would be the last sound they heard in this life. No wonder they were brutalised. Recruited under the pretence of being auxiliaries to the Royal Irish Constabulary, Ireland must have seemed to be a cushy posting until bullets ripped from the hedgerows and the roads erupted beneath their lorries. That was when they should have been withdrawn, when it was perfectly clear they were not wanted in this place. But governments do not personally have to fight wars. They can afford to bluster and threaten from a safe distance while other men die at their bidding. And violence begets violence in even the most moderate of men.

That was the Irishman in him, the man whose taproot went straight down to the life-giving water beneath the house where he was born, the man whose voice was overlaid with something which caused Irish heads to turn in his direction whenever he spoke abroad. Yet while he thought with loathing of the brutes who killed and pillaged in the King's name the lineal Englishman who was the other half of his Ascendancy inheritance argued that they were no worse than the equally

118

brutal men who opposed them without showing their faces to the light of day and reminded him that it was <u>his</u> ancestors who first raised the flag of rebellion here in Ireland as they did in America and everywhere where there was injustice to be fought.

But was it really and truly injustice? For the majority of both peoples life was hard and unfair either side of the Irish Sea, so that was not it. What it was - it came to him slowly but unmistakably - was the insolent belief that they were incapable of ruling themselves. That was it. Insolence. No wonder they were angered to the point of armed rebellion. Any nation would feel the same way.

His dead father's voice, the voice of his brother and the rasping voice of little Reggie Barrie accused him from beyond their graves, mocking him for harbouring thoughts verging on treachery. Everything he had been taught to hold sacred was colliding against the tortured extremities of his own mind. Still he felt that he was a man and should be able to make up his own mind - as he was in fact doing now. Separate the grain from the chaff or mix them how you will the fact remained that these men who called themselves the Irish Republican Army were fighting simply for the right to self-determination and not for any material gain for themselves. It was now or never for this fledgling Army. There was a growing feeling that it would be a bloody fight. A conflict with the Empire was ever thus. At the least they were deserving of his sympathy, and if it was not for the hurt it would cause to his mother and Constance he would be strongly inclined to join with them.

He heard his mother's voice anxiously calling his name and went back inside the house with old Sheila faithfully padding along at his heels.

EIGHT

Young Eileen gagged as she was stirring the big stockpot on the edge of the stove. Then she ran from the kitchen clutching her mouth while Mrs Comiskey watched her sourly. Cook had been suspicious of that young lady before now with her slipping out every time that no-good Seamus Fogarty passed the window and him looking like he wasn't doing it on purpose. If she had her way, a Catholic would never be employed within the four walls of any decent Protestant house for they were well known to be an immoral lot and you only had to look at the families they had to realise the truth of that. Down in the village there was one poor woman with fourteen children...fourteen! And the woman herself not yet forty though if truth be told she looked at least twice that. Like animals they were.

It had been a big mistake on Mrs Aylmer's part ever to let the girl inside the door, for them kind didn't know what gratitude was and she had never known a family yet to employ a Catholic indoors without having cause to regret it. And it wasn't very nice for the rest of the staff. People who worked for people of quality had their own positions to keep up and it was lowering for them to have to work alongside an unwashed slip of a girl who didn't know enough to pull the chain after she'd used the lavatory and who received every well-meant comment on her work with a loud braying like she was an ass or something. What life could be like in the Mangan home with six of them all packed in together she could not imagine but it showed in them, in the strong animal smell they carried about with them and in their filthy eating habits. Poor Mrs Aylmer was too soft-hearted for her own good, so she was. Better she got a good Protestant girl down from Dublin or even Belfast if she wanted a kitchenmaid for there was plenty who would be more than glad of the job.

'Are y'all right now then?' she asked as Eileen returned to the kitchen, out of breath and her eyes red with retching and the soft bloom of maternity already on her childish face so that the formidable Mrs Comiskey felt sorry for her and truly wished she could make herself feel more kindly towards this unwanted interloper in her sacred domain.

Eileen grunted a reply which was probably 'Yes' but without any thanks for the enquiry and Mrs Comiskey thought there's no doubt about it now, that girl is in trouble all right. And she really should report it to Mrs Aylmer but didn't like to because the old lady was in such low health with all that had been happening around Ardnagoilte in the past weeks. But someone would have to be told. And soon. Properly speaking her mother should be the one to know that her daughter was pregnant and could not be allowed to remain in this kitchen for much longer, but there was no power in the world great enough to make Cook break such news to the washerwoman who was known to one and all has having the most scalding tongue in the parish. Maybe Miss Constance. Maybe Miss Constance would be the one to tell and then she could tell the mistress if she liked. In any event it would shift the responsibility from her own shoulders.

That was the weekend of the Pattern when people came on foot and by donkey cart from outlying farms and villages to help Gorteen celebrate the feast day of its patron saint. With all its faults the Catholic church does not require the faithful to be unnecessarily miserable after religious obligations have been properly discharged and thinks nothing if its children spend the rest of the day in games and innocent enjoyment. For how else could it be said to be a celebration of anything.

At the end of the Mass, and in honour of the day that was in it, Benediction, the most beautiful ceremony in the liturgy of the church, was given to invoke the blessing of Almighty God on this parish and its people. Burdened by the sacred vestments, layers of them heavily embroidered with gold thread, Father Gilligan laboured up the three steps to Calvary, performing his priestly office by habit, placing the white wafer which was God in the centre of the gold sunburst monstrance and placing it on the altar facing the congregation for their adoration.

It had all happened so often before. The 'Tantun Ergo' and the 'O Salutaris Hostia', the sweet smelling incense wafting about him and then the Divine Praises with the strong, confident responses from choir and people who knew through the certainty of their blood that their God was truly present here on the altar in Gorteen.

And through it all, through clouds of sickly incense and the sound of four hundred voices raised in the paean which had been their forefathers' for centuries Father Gilligan was sick and tired at heart for the dreadful things which had been happening all over Ireland for years past and which now appeared in Wicklow - even here in Gorteen - as a manifestation of the Devil himself. For Father Gilligan believed in the Devil as surely as he believed in God. Why the Almighty allowed Satan to work his evil on simple people he did not understand, accepting that it was so for doubting was in itself in the nature of a sin. 'God's ways are not our ways' he told himself for the thousandth time. 'Blessed be the holy will of God.'

Outside the chapel people who had not seen each other for the best part of a year quickly forgot the commonplace miracle of God come on earth and greeted each other soberly and formed distinct groups, the women surrounded by children as an island is surrounded by the sea and the men idling their way round the back of Byrne's public house to share a few convivial pints of frothing stout in a companionable silence. One of the few remarks which would be made - and it would be made several times by various men as their sole contribution to the conversation - would be that patterns were not what they used to be, remembering perhaps when they had fought barefisted for honour alone or sidled up to a girl and dared start a dialogue which would end up in a couple of years time with Father Peter himself joining them in holy wedlock. For he was held to be a very lucky priest with marriages, and how could it be otherwise when it was known to one and all that he was a saint on earth. No trouble ever came from one of Father Peter's marriages and there was never a shortage of children and all of them in the best of health, praise be to God.

On the edge of the village a lush-grassed field had been set aside each year for the celebrations. Strange looking families had arrived overnight in rickety carts and wagons to set up their stalls for the trade which would arrive after the Sunday dinner had been eaten. Swarthy, thin-nosed men with their billowing wives and hordes of dark-eyed children who moved week by week according to a calendar of their own to towns and villages throughout the land where there would be a fair or a pattern, coming from nowhere and disappearing into nowhere as the mists of the surrounding hills. Thimblerriggers and trick-of-the-loop men, the proprietor of a manpowered roundabout and a pair of swingboats, a hoop-la stall and another stall where at a cost of three wooden balls for twopence a blade could perhaps smash a penny reject plate and win a pipe-cleaner monkey bought at five shillings the gross together with the admiration of the bystanders, and the garishly painted van of the ice cream man who had chugged out bright and early from Arklow to show his Neapolitan brood at Mass for luck.

By tomorrow morning all would be gone as mysteriously as they had arrived. Just now they were gathered by their own separate cooking fires watched by small boys defying their mothers' warning that the gypsies might steal them, as if they had any shortage of children of their own. At the far end of the field H-shaped goal-posts had been erected for the prime event of the day which would be the annual camogie match between the ladies of Gorteen and Gortmore. If past form was any indication they would very soon forget all about pucking the hard leather ball through their opponent's goal and do battle in earnest with their tin-bound hurley sticks. And it would be a very lucky woman indeed who escaped with nothing worse than four inches of skin lifted from her shin although as far as living memory went no one had ever actually been killed on the field of play.

Shrieks of excitement like snatches of music heard from afar came to Rory's ears as he strode down the road from

Ardnagoilte with old Sheila padding along patiently behind, and at the sound he hastened his step. It was only half an hour earlier when he decided impulsively that it was a chance to become more identified with his villagers and supposed he would just arrive at the pattern and move around exchanging greeting with anyone he happened to know well enough. Otherwise he would just keep himself decently in the background and maybe in time they would become used to seeing him among them. Then perhaps he would become more closely involved in the life of the village which had been his home since the day he was born.

It was nothing like that. At the gate a man wearing a green rosette and with a battered Gladstone bag suspended by string across his chest was taking the entrance money. When Rory said 'Hello, Duggan!' and offered him a shilling the man started visibly and said hastily 'Jaysus, Misthur Aylmer. Sure I can't very well charge ya for enterin' yer own field' and nothing would make him take the coin.

Inside it was no better. Men he addressed by name looked embarrassed and touched their caps sullenly or went silent or moved away out of earshot so that even poor old Sheila sensed she was on alien ground and pressed herself nervously against his leg. Then a man bawling through a cardboard megaphone announced the start of the children's' races and people surged towards the playing area for the last events of the day. Gortmore won the tug-of-war easily and were jeered for it. Sundry children, barefoot for speed, panted along with their arms flailing like little windmills in so many desperate attempts to win the certificate which would adorn the mantleshelves of their homes until time and woodsmoke destroyed these mementoes of a brief glory. Then, amid shrill partisan cat-calling the rival camogie teams took the field, not in playing gear for none of them had any but with the jerseys of the mans' football teams pulled anyway over their dresses to show which village they had the honour to represent. The game began in a flurry of hurley-sticks with the referee keeping a safe distance between himself and the players who right from the beginning lashed out indiscriminately at anyone nearby.

Father Gilligan had put in his token appearance and taken himself off home to settle down with the newspaper, for he was a man who had no wish to hamper the enjoyment of his parishioners and experience had taught him there were times when it was best for all concerned if he did not actually see what was happening. But Father O'Reilly remained, the centre of a little cluster of men who showed no interest whatever for the game. Cries of 'Get the Thackaberry wan!' and 'Send them back ta Gartmore' rose from the sidelines with wild whooping and the clash of stout ash hurleys from the field of play and the mournful bray of a neglected donkey as Rory approached the little knot of men gathered around the young priest.

'I wonder what brings our young squireen among the commonality taday' remarked Derry Keogh as he caught sight of the tweeded figure with the old dog at his side coming towards them. Then 'you two better make yerselves scarce' and two of the men melted into the crowd and became suddenly engrossed in the game. Derry said 'We don't often see you here, Misther Aylmer' as Rory stopped and wished them all a good day, each by name for apart from Father O'Reilly there were all in some way employees of his.

Rory answered 'I though it might be a good idea to show my face at the Pattern. After all, we all live in the same village.'

'Well there's some that do and some that don't' said Keogh meaningfully while the young priest looked over his head and resolved not to answer the man if he was spoken to directly. This was a Catholic function. No one but a Protestant would have had the arrogance to intrude this way. It was typical of the breed to force themselves where they were not wanted. But there would come an end to that and the sooner the better.

'It seems to be going very well' remarked Rory, not even aware that his very presence here was an affront to the people he was among.

'Ah, we can manage ta run things ourselves all right' Keogh said with heavy sarcasm. 'Little things like a patteren, ya understand, Misther Aylmer. Big things, like running' the countery an' that, well we're not quite up ta that yet. But we'll learn. Y'can take me word fer that, we'll learn all right' and in his own mind he added 'when we've seen the lasta you an' yer like' while the others looked in admiration of the repartee which was passing over this ignorant shoneen's head.

For all the bland smiles Rory felt he was not altogether welcome among the. Why he could not say for they were all of them so deferential, more deferential than he wished anyone to be to him, but maybe they were just ill at ease in his company. After another few remarks all received with the same pretended attention he moved away wondering why none of the indoor staff at Ardnagoilte seemed to be present.

'You gev him something to think about there, Derry, all right' said the young priest, smiling tight-lipped and Derry answered with satisfaction 'He can put that in his pipe and smoke it. How'd he like it if we invited ourselves to wanna them garden parties at the big house? An' willya just lookit him now, makin' upta the widda Mangan like a proper little gentleman showin' how de-mo-cratic he is', keeping a guard on his tongue in the presence of the curate who dearly wanted to be known as the 'rebel priest' like Father Flanaghan back in Sixteen and who did not particularly care what language Derry used as long as it was not blasphemous, for it would be the people who provoked it who would have to bear the blame in the sight of God.

'An it's yerself is it, Misther Rory' asked Lizzie Mangan, wondering uneasily if the young master recognised the socks she was wearing or if maybe he'd missed that yoke young Eileen was wearing for bloomers now she was putting on weight from eating too much at the big house. 'sure it's a grand day that's in it, thanks bitta God. An' it's well an' illigant yer lookin' yerself' noticing the good suit of Donegal tweed with the cap to match and the fine heavy boots that wouldn't let in water in a month of Sundays.

Rory smiled and touched his cap which made her primp with pride that one of the gentry should be touching his cap to her in the sight of all Gorteen. That'd make them see what class've

a person Lizzie Mangan was, quickly glancing around to
anyone was noticing it. But they were all too engrossed in
mayhem being perpetrated between the ladies of Gorteen
Gortmore as the battle between the villages became for the
moment smaller and more bitter battles between persons.

'How is Larry?' Rory asked. 'Is he working?'

'Ah divil a bit've workin' is in it' she replied bitterly. 'Sure
there's nothin' around here for a lad except maybe a few days
for the Council' thinking wildly that if she played her cards
right maybe young Misther Aylmer would put in a good word
with Herselff and get her darling Larry taken on at the big
house.

'Well, if you ask him to call at the house I think we have some
work in the garden he could do' said Rory casually and Lizzie
Mangan was instantly in seventh heaven. Workin' at the big
house! Larry'd be set up for life so he would. Never look back
again he wouldn't. And she swiftly surveyed all her recent
intercessions and decided that Saint Jude should have the credit
for this minor miracle. Either him or Saint Anthony or the Little
Flower for all of them had been mobilised in Larry's cause and
if it cost a few pence in candles what of it. With both Larry and
Eileen earning they could afford a thanksgiving candle for all
three and another for the Holy Mother of God under whose
protection she had placed her entire family.

Touching his cap again Rory smiled vaguely at a few people
nearby and stepped along the village street thinking how
utterly wrong the poor old Admiral had been about these
people. Like a voice in the rustling hedgerow he could hear
his old friend warning 'You can't afford to trust them for they
are the most dangerous of liars. They believe their own lies.
They make up their own history. They tell you England was
responsible for the famine until you begin to believe it yourself
although you know that it was an Act of God and that it was
only the poorest of peasants who suffered. For the priests, the
shopkeepers, the professional classes and the town dwellers
lived through it quite comfortably without even thinking of
raising a hand to help the men, women and children starving

on their doorsteps. To listen to them you would think the British government imported the potato blight just to kill off the Irish. The truth is they were just lazy people growing a lazy crop and when it failed they had to blame someone other than themselves or their God. Listen to them long enough and you'll become as bad as them yourself.'

Poor Admiral Barry, as ignorant as the peasants in his own bigoted way, reared in fear of the masses at his gate and growing more fearful with age and change until he somehow provoked the attack which cost him his life, whoever it was to blame. The Black and Tans? Most likely, for they were well known for that sort of thing. But the men of Gorteen...never. You only had to speak to them to understand what good chaps they were at heart. Poor uncle Reggie had got it all wrong.

Back at the dying Pattern Derry said again 'I still wonder what brought him an' that oul' dog a his inta the village taday.' The rebel priest who saw himself on horseback at the head of a peasant army advancing implacably on Dublin Castle said softly 'Maybe he's a spy, come to see what he could find out. He wouldn't be the first ex-officer turned informer' adding irrelevantly 'Thinks more of that old dog than the poor souls who serve at his table, so he does. The English are a queer class've a people. Think more of dogs than their fellow men.'

NINE

'Wait till ya hear what I've gotta tell ya' said the widow, out of breath with excitement coming through the half-open door to where Larry was sitting before the smouldering fire and him with a face like a week of wet Sundays.

 Something had happened again inside his trousers, something he couldn't tell his mother or even the priest for he had enjoyed it too much to be anything less than mortal sin. And it wasn't the first or the second time either. Sometimes it happened during the night and then he lay awake waiting for it and praying fervently to his guardian angel not to let it happen. For it frightened the life out of him and he did not want to go to hell for something he could not help.

The widow noticed nothing and if she had it would have meant little against the great news she was bringing to her most precious son. 'Yer ta start worrk at the big house in the mornin' she told him, a little disappointed that his excitement did not match her own. 'Got it from Misther Rory hisself I did. Kem upta me nice as ya like at the Pattern an' raised his cap ta me before everrywan, called me 'Mrs Mangan' like he'd never seen me toilin' an' moilin' all weathers in the wash-house like I was quality same as hisself he did. 'Mrs Mangan' he says, polite as ya like but then the quality is like that when ya getta know them. 'Mrs Mangan, an' how is me old friend an' playmate Larry?' So I tells him yer in the besta forrum an' the next thing he says is 'Is he workin' yet?' So a course I hasta tell him divil a work is in it except the roads an' no sonna mine is ever gointa be found sittin' dead on a heaps stones like his poor ould father, God rest him. Then he says 'Yer quite right, Mrs Mangan. Larry's too good a boy ta be wasted on them kinda jobs so if ya send him upta the house in the mornin' he can start work in the gardens rightaway'. Now isn't that the verry best news ya ever heard in yer whole life? A steady job with the Aylmers an' y'll never look back, an' may God an' His Blessed Mother bless them for it. Sure I've always said there's nothin' like the oul' gentry for helpin' the workin' classes so I have. We're blessed in Gorteen with the Aylmers, an' nowan betther let me be hearin' wan word agen them' and she glared at the smoke-dimmed walls as if they would dare contradict her.

Larry was not as impressed as she had expected when she ran all the way home from the village bearing the glad tidings and completely forgetting that she had gone to the pattern primarily to see the gerrls didn't get in bad company. For even though they were the finest gerrls any woman could ever wish to have there was a few quare fellas only waitin' their chance to turn their heads with soft words and have their will of them before returning to Arklow or Gortmore for never a Gorteen man would even dream of taking advantage of a poor innocent girl, and that was the God's honest truth.

'What'll I haveta do there?' asked Larry as he considered what category of sin he might have committed but certain that it must be the worst possible, the kind oul' Father Pether was always goin' on about at the ten o'clock Mass although no one was every very sure what he was getting at. To Father Gilligan the only sin worth wasting a sermon on was the one he heard most of in confession, what he called 'the sins of the flesh' and leaving his parishioners to draw their own conclusions: the ones who committed them would know what he was referring to and the others, the children and backward adults, would find out in their own good time. Anyway it was not a subject to be mentioned openly anywhere and least all within the house of God.

'Amn't I only afther tellin' ya?' demanded the widow. 'Work in the gardens, that's what Misther Rory said. Sure they haven't had annywan regular since that oul' Scotchman MacIver left so there's yer chance. Worrk hard an' get the garden lookin' like a new pin an' yer there for life. Maybe Herself'll let us move inta MacIver's House' she hazarded as a vista of roses and tea from proper cups and a roof which never leaked filled her mind like an opium eater's dream. The gerrls would have a room ta theirselves an' Larry would have his an' she would have the bed to herself an' they would have one room for eatin' in an' another just for sittin' like the quality theirselves. They'd even have a little room fer washin' an' a lavvertery with a chain to pull instead of squatting in the bracken behind the cottage in all weathers. The splendour of her vision was dazzling and she thought how good God had been to bless her with a fine, strapping son whom everyone liked and how none of them would ever look back from this day forward. A novena of thanks, that's what she would make. A novena of thanks to Our Lady of Lourdes and Saint Jude and Saint Anthony and the Little Flower and to every other impressed saint in her heavenly battalion who might have changed the lives of all the Mangans by this most momentous of miracles.

'Sure I don't know annythin' about gardenin' Larry repeated sullenly and for a moment all her bright dreams lay shattered about her feet.

'Evverywan knows about gardens' she told him crossly. 'All ya haveta do is cut the grass an' stick things in the ground an' they grow up same like the praties. Annywan can do it, an' if an iggerant oul' Protestan like MacIver could do it then my Larry can do it twice as well. Ten times as well' she added generously.

'I don't know' Larry protested weakly. He liked the vision of himself in the rarefied atmosphere of the big house eating as much jam sponge as he liked the way Eileen said they did and he fancied the thought of being an employed man with a respectable occupation to make the village look up to him instead of treatin' him as some class've an eejit. But it frightened him to think he would have to leave his mother's house every morning and spend the rest of the day among strangers. And, though he had so far only seen her from a distance, he had a positive dread of old Mrs Aylmer. From what Eileen said all the servants went in dread of the old lady so the less he had to do with the likes of her the happier would be. But he would be seeing Rory again. Maybe they'd even work in the garden together when they weren't out finding a fox's earth or maybe catching collickers under the bridge. Gradually he was becoming accustomed to the idea of working but he could not help wishing that something - something painless, of course -

would take the oul' melt before she kem giving him the edge of her tongue the way Eileen said she did to the others.

His mother was adamant. 'There's many a grown man with a family ta keep'd give his right hand for the chance yer getting' she told him. 'A job fer life an' all the food ya kin ate whenever ya wanta ate it. It's on yer knees ya should be this minnit thinking' all the saints in heaven that Misther Rory put in a good worrd for ya with the oul' wan. Sure it'll be the makin' of yer. Yer the luckiest boy in all Gorteen so y'are. Here. Come an' see what yer Mammy has for ya' and she drew him into the back rooms and reached beneath the bed to pull out a cardboard box. 'Now what d'ya thinka that, me fine bucko?' displaying the tweed suit. Rumpled and all that it was it was still the finest suit of clothes Larry had ever seen. 'Is that fer me, Mammy?' he asked.

'Of course it's fer you, who else'd it be for? That's wanna Misther Rory's best suits so it is. The oul' wan gev it ta me but I thought ta meself 'I'll not show this ta Larry just yet, I'll wait till I can give him the whole outfit like when he was makin' his Confirmation so I will.' Here's a cap ta go with it an' as good a paira boots as yever clapped eyes on. Two shillin's I gev for them boots ta Waxie Connolly. Kem from a big house in Dubelin he said, an' the soles an' heels are the best Kerry leather so they are. Ya kin wear them boots year in an' year out an' nevver a droppa wather'll they let in. Now put on yer new clothes an' let yer Mammy see her luvvely son. Go on. Put them on fer yer Mammy.'

When Larry had been cajoled into changing into his finery she regarded him with a touching satisfaction and sighed 'If only yer poor father could see ya now its prouda his son he'd be for it's a picture y'are. Sure if you an' Misther Rory was standin' side by side an' someone hadta pick out the gentleman it's you they would be pickin' as a large tear eased itself from her eye and rolled unhindered down her careworn cheek and all for the memory of a man who could do no more than break stones for his living.

Recovering herself she said briskly 'First thing in the mornin' ya wash yer face proper. None've yer lick-an-a-promise mind, wash it proper with soap an' a clane towel an' get yerself dressed in yer new suit an' go right upta the house an' tell Mrs Aylmer yer thanks fer givin' ya the job. Then ya come back here an' change inta yer oul' rags fer workin'. But first of all ya thank that good woman fer givin' ya the best chance yever had in yer life because them sort get great store on good manners, so see ya behave yerself. Now, tell me what yer goin' ta say when yer taken in ta see the mistress? Go on, tell me. What're ya goin' ta say t' her thats been so good ta ya, better than annya yer own'd be, the trash.'

Larry looked not a bit like Mister Rory as he stood before his mother with his jacket hanging from his shoulders and the trousers sagging about his legs and the brand new cap perched on his head as if it had fallen there from space. His big girlish face showed bewilderment and for a moment it looked as if he might break into crying for the effort of it all. He knew that his Mammy was right and that he was being given the chance of a lifetime. Yet he could not help wishing that none of it had ever happened, that he could have gone on trapping linnets to set them loose again or watch the unvarying ritual of the rabbits at morn and eventide.

The widow Mangan knew her son. Knew too that given half a chance he would find some very good reason why he should not present himself before the great lady of the big house and so lose this heaven sent opportunity for bettering them all. MacIver's house she knew well, a fine brickbuilt place on the other side of the estate where they had all them glasshouses and vegetable garden and the trees which kept the house supplied with fruit all the year round. Oul' Mrs MacIver was living there still but she could not last much longer and even if she did there was sure to be some saint whose business it was to transfer unwanted tenants to another place: without hurting them, for that would be bad. She could see herself properly dressed in a coat which had never belonged to anyone else and the gerrls proper little ladies in gingham with sidebutton boots and all of them so well-mannered that it would be the wonder of the parish. Sunday mornings she would lead her family to the chapel and they would pay twopence each and rub shoulders with the wives of the grocer and the publican and the National School teacher in the select section directly before the altar where there was a bit of carpet on the floor and you could always be first up to Communion and never have to queue like the common people.

'Now take them clothes off an' let me put them away proper' she said gruffly to hide her emotions. It only needed one of them to start it and they would both be crying their heads off when the gerrls came home from the pattern. 'Now say 'Thanks fer givin' me the job, Mrs Aylmer' an' don't ferget ta take yer cap off. An' kape yer hands outa yer pockets fer them kind set great store on things like that. Go on, say it. Say 'Thanks fer givin' me the job, Mrs Aylmer.' An' don't wipe yer nose on yer sleeve. Go on, say it. Say 'Thanks fer givin' me the job, Mrs Aylmer.' An' spake up. There's nothin' ta be afraid of.

Larry looked at her sullenly. Then he burst into tears.

'Well I think it was most unwise ' said Lavinia Aylmer. 'They simply do not want us take an interest in their affairs. Your father tried that many years ago and was laughed at for his pains. Look what they did to Parnell. Turned against him over a slip of a girl decent people would not have allowed inside their doors. It was the priests behind it, of course. The priests did not like the idea of the people following a Protestant. So they denounced him from the pulpit and you know the Irish, more afraid of the priests than of death itself. We knew Charles Parnell, you know. Dined often at Avondale and he has dined with us. And at Iveraun. Of course that was before he became so enamoured of Home Rule for Ireland and turned his back on all his old friends, so in a way I suppose you could say it served him right. But he was a very charming man, and honourable as the day.'

Constance's pale oval face brightened with interest. 'Did you actually know Mrs O'Shea? she asked and the old lady sniffed most eloquently. 'I did not' she answered. 'Nor would I have wished to. In those days we were very careful about choosing our friends.'

'Maybe that was the trouble' suggested Rory. 'Or part of it anyway. Maybe we should have made more of an effort to get to know them. Maybe we should have involved ourselves more.'

'I have already told you they don't want us to be involved' explained the old lady impatiently. 'They simply do not want it and personally I think they are quite right for we could never have any common ground.'

'I don't know' said Rory doubtfully. 'I thought they were quite charming and friendly.'

'To the master of Ardnagoilte! Of course they were charming and friendly...to your face. Behind your back it would be a different story, you can take my word on that. These people hate us that what we are - no, for being what they are not. They hate us because we made estates from waste land and built houses when they didn't even know how to roof a cottage. I have lived a long time in this country, too long maybe. And I can tell you from my own experience that the ruling passion of the Irish is nothing less than envy naked and unashamed. That was what did for Charles Parnell, you know. You can forget the 'Uncrowned King of Ireland' title. What they could not forgive was that he was a Protestant landowner, what I believe they call the Ascendancy. Had he been a Catholic he could have had a dozen Kitty O'Sheas and no one would have turned a hair. You are a man now, Rory, and quite old enough to make up your own mind. But if you will be guided by an old woman who is very concerned for your welfare you will keep your distance as far as Gorteen is concerned.'

'Maybe your mother is right' suggested Constance anxiously. 'After all, she does know what she is talking about.'

'Of course I am right' snapped Lavinia. 'Reggie Barry was right but he would have been much better holding his tongue about it. People of our generation understood things better. If I call a servant by her surname it is because I know that if I call her 'Biddy' or 'Mary' she will be calling me Lavinia in no time

135

at all. And then we will be having cosy chats and I shall be the mistress no longer. Standards have to be maintained. Once they are allowed to slip they just go on falling and Charles Parnell is a very good example of that. It is much better for everyone if they keep their own place in society. On second thoughts I do not think I will have the Mangan boy in the garden after all. One Mangan in the house is quite enough, for that is another thing you have to watch. One brings another and in no time at all the house is full of them and all of them conspiring behind your back.'

'I'm afraid I've already told him' confessed Rory. 'I saw Mrs Mangan at the Pattern and I told her she could send young Larry up to start in the garden tomorrow. I thought that was what you wanted.'

'Well in that case we shall just have to let him start' said the old lady dubiously. 'It need not be for long, just long enough to get the weeds under control and after that we will see. The one thing one must never do is to break one's word however unadvisedly it may have been given. Because they are all born liars is no reason why we should lie too. Anyway I doubt if he will come. Clearing weeds is very hard work and they are not very fond of that. Mind you, the mother is a hard worker. Not a good worker but a very hard one if only she would stop stealing small things, but one must expect that. I have always thought there must be tinker blood in that family, or maybe too much in-breeding. Something anyway. But since you have given your word we had better let the boy come. Maybe he will surprise us all. Sometimes very simple men are very good with plants. Anyway he cannot do a lot of harm with the weeds.'

In the world beyond Gorteen tremendous things were happening, such things as no Irishman had ever thought to be really possible even with the assistance of all the saints in heaven. For the sun of empire had passed its zenith and had already commenced its inevitable descent to the far horizon, below which it would disappear never to rise again. Over the water in England well-intentioned men told each other that the persecution of the Irish had gone on for far too long or that the place was not worth fighting for. But in the pubs and the Sinn Fein clubs, in backstreet hide-outs and on lonely hillsides hunted men looked on each other in a wild amaze and said jubilantly that the Big Fellow had pulled it off and that England had been fought to a standstill. For why else would Lloyd George of all people agree to a Truce and invite the outlawed Irish to send a delegation to Downing Street to consider terms for a Treaty to end the fighting forever and abandon Ireland to Irish rule, a thing no other leader had ever come in spitting distance of doing.

Now the men of the IRA could flaunt themselves openly. And flaunt they did, holding church parades of bedraggled and unmilitary soldiers in civilian clothes who found it difficult to march in step but who nevertheless paraded with the confidence of the conquerors which they most assuredly were. Men who had carefully distanced themselves from the rebels for reasons of policy now hastened to mend fences against the possibility of the wrath to come or at least to be in on the ground floor of the new enterprise: for to the man of business profit is always profit wherever it comes from.

For an agonizing time the issue hung in the balance as Collins, Griffith, Barton and Childers travelled weekly between Dublin and London to discuss matters which could not be spoken of over the then primitive telephone system while de Valera exercised his veto from Dublin insisting that he would personally not be satisfied with anything less than a republic for all of Ireland, including the recalcitrant province of Ulster with its two million fanatically loyal Protestants and Lloyd George boxed as clever as he knew how to salvage something from the wreckage. In time Griffith, whose position before the events of 1916 had been simply for a measure of Home Rule, and Collins, the smiling man of steel whose ragtail army had forced mighty England to the conference table, had enough of toing and froing and quibbles over unimportant things so they took responsibility upon themselves by signing a Treaty which the majority of the people back home thought to be a good bargain, for to them the Republic was only a word first heard in Easter Week and life was too hard to be splitting hairs over what most of them saw as being no more than trifles.

Father Gilligan read the newspaper reports and thanked God that sense and decency had returned to Ireland again, that no more would men of whom none knew of any evil be shot dead on their own doorsteps to unleash the fury of the Black and Tans in raids of reprisal. As an Irishman he was pleased that his country was recovering its ancient dignity among the nations of the earth, had already recovered it in fact for never before had the invincible British empire sued for peace, which in effect was what they had done by proposing a Truce in the first place. Father O'Reilly was so euphoric that he gave a sermon in Irish which few but himself in the chapel could understand for the days of the language revival were still some way off. But it was a gesture he much enjoyed as indeed did his uncomprehending congregation.

Not everyone in Gorteen was immediately pleased. Tortuous and time consuming as the London negotiations were it was all happening too fast while there were still many outstanding scores to be settled. But they knew their leader. When Collins ordered 'Cease fire' he meant it.

'Well, its now or never, boys' said Captain Derry Keogh as he replaced his empty stout glass on the marble counter of the pub. Before him three other glasses awaited his pleasure and he had forgotten how many he already had for suddenly he was the most popular man in the village with, it seemed, everyone anxious to buy a drink for the local hero who stood surrogate for the adored Collins. 'We shoulda done it the night we did Iveraun so we should.'

'Ah sure the oul' wan'd never be got outa the house' said one man weekly. 'The pooer oul' bitch can't walk a step without help. She'd a been burrned ta death so she would.'

'Well what of it?' demanded Keogh, his natural anger fuelled by the drinks he had denied himself while he was 'on active service.' 'It'd have been one less Sassenach in Gorteen. An' what about what they did to our women with their rapin' an' killin' an' all sortsa unnatural practices? What about that? Sure burnin's too good for them.'

'Never had anny've that in Gorteen nor in Wickla as far's I've heard' said Sean sulkily. 'As far as Gorteen is concerned they've always been decent people.'

'Ah willya shut yer face' retorted Keogh. 'Sure we all knew it was happenin' all over the country, an' worse if it wasn't all hushed up be the Castle. I say the man's a spy and no spy is goin' ta walk away free while I'm the Captain've Gorteen. I say we do it now or first thing in the mornin' before this Treatya theirs becomes official. Annywan that isn't with us is agen us. An' nonea them is with us, that's the surest thing ya can count on. By tomorra Aylmer'll be dead even if I haveta do it on me own. I'd do it now only I'm in no condition to shoot straight. Well, we can't let all this stout go to waste. So drink up, boys, an' to hell with England!'

With which they all agreed. So it happened that as Larry Mangan in his secondhand finery walked from the porch of Ardnagoilte after an audience with Herself who was, he thought in amazement, not such a bad oul' stick at all, a ragged volley of rifle fire rang out from the plantation and he was dead even before he began to wonder what the noise was.

'It was you they were after' said Lavinia when the lifeless body was carried back into the house and taken to the staff hall to await the arrival of priest, police and doctor in that order. 'No one would have any reason for shooting young Mangan and he was wearing your old suit. It was you they were after' she said again 'so you can see for yourself how friendly they are. His poor mother' she went on, remembering the desolation which had entered her own life when the news of Andrew's death came in a buff envelope delivered by an army despatch rider in recognition of the family's privileged position in the eyes of Dublin Castle. On that never to be forgotten day she had cursed God even though she still had one son left, for the bond between a mother and her firstborn is older than the earth and stronger than passion. Maybe poor Mrs Mangan would find the strength from her religion that she had failed to find in hers. 'She will have to be told' she ended, trying to rise from the prison of her chair.

'I'll go down and see her' offered Rory. 'I'll go' said Constance 'or maybe we could go together. She may take it badly.'

'She will do that alright' said Lavinia bitterly, for what could men know of an anguish which starts in the womb. 'I will go and break it to her. It may come better from another mother and its the least I can do. The boy was killed on our ground. Tell Nolan to bring round the dog cart and help me out of this chair. I'll go alone if you don't mind' anticipating Constance's offer to accompany her on a mission which would be both distasteful and distressing but which as the mistress of Ardnagoilte it was plainly her duty to undertake.

'Please obliged me by getting my cloak and hat, Constance. Then help me on to the porch. I will take her...no, better not take her anything. A woman who has just lost her only son will be past consoling. But you can ask the doctor to follow me down in about half on hour in case she needs his attention. My cloak and hat, please, Constance.'

Constance hurried upstairs and Rory went out calling to Nolan to bring round the dog cart. But wherever he was Nolan was not answering, so Rory went to the stables himself and yoked the pony and cart. Then he led it round to the front of the house where his mother was waiting so calm and white-lipped that he wondered at her fortitude and realised that this was a woman he loved very much as well as respecting her. Together with Constance and the old dog he stood on the gravelled drive and watched the little diligence proceed sedately toward the village, wishing he had gone with her but knowing that this was something she had to do alone, for to people like Lavinia Aylmer responsibility and duty were synonymous. To her generation rank did indeed confer obligations which could never be avoided however unpleasant or dangerous, wondering too if when the time came he would

140

find the same courage within himself.

Bad news always travels fast and nowhere more than in Ireland where it seems to be carried in the wind or on the wings of swallows. Before Lavinia carefully guided the pony through the massive gateway old Mrs Whitmore peered anxiously through her lodge window and prayed earnestly that no more trouble would come upon the house, suddenly aware that she was alien by both race and religion and that the small lodge which was her home was a very vulnerable place to be.

Kneeling on the earth floor of her cottage the widow Mangan scooped handfuls of ash from the fireplace and smeared it on her face and hair as she keened her misery. With a grasping movement of her right hand she plucked God and all his saints from her heart, ready to sell her very soul to the Devil if she could see Larry come through the door again, whimpering like a wounded animal as she reasoned with unanswerable logic that if A had not happened then B would not have happened so the person who caused A was responsible for B, C and D. It was the oul' wan who asked Larry to go to the big house, so she had killed him. Even among the most intelligent grief cries for relief and with the least intelligent revenge on almost anyone becomes an imperative when a mother's world has come to an end. And she had done nothing about the thatch in all those months.

She heard the light clop of the pony's hooves and the slurred sound of the wheels coming to an unhurried stop at the foot of the bank outside. The impertinence of it nearly took her breath away. Nowan but oul' Aylmer would have the face to call on a mother after killing their son but that was the class of people they were. All of Ireland was their playground and the Irish no more than toys to be discarded once they were broken. And if there was a god in heaven at all the old bitch and all belonging to her should be struck dead on the spot.

Lavinia reined in the pony and braced herself for the ordeal ahead. Already the painfully rehearsed words of condolence were becoming jumbled in her mind as she told herself that her distress could be as nothing compared with what the poor woman inside the cottage would feel when the dreadful news had been broken to her. But it had to be faced for decency's sake and it might be a help coming from someone who had known the same desolating sorrow.

'Mrs Mangan!' she called very genteely, for ladies never ever raised their voices in any circumstances. Then more stridently, as was her manner, 'Mrs Mangan!' and thinking again of her opening words about being very sorry to be the bearer of bad news and all the other meaningless phrases which are all mankind has in its pitiful armoury against life's greatest test. The pony pawed the roadway and ignored the lush grass of the bank as some instinct warned of imminent danger to set her flanks quivering with fear while behind her on the cushioned cross-seat of the car Lavinia fiddled nervously with the buttons of her gloves and again steeled herself to face the anguish of a bereaved mother with whom she at this moment felt the deepest affinity.

The quiet of the treelined lane was abruptly broken and birds rose squawking in alarmed chorus as a shrieking, ash-smeared fiend shrieking erupted through the doorway of the tumbledown cottage. Whinnying and skittering in panic the pony reared up and dashed headlong down the hill and into the village street to cause pandemonium among women gossiping at their doorways and make them reach fearfully for children playing their mysterious games in the roadway. Then the wreckage of the cart spun round and round on the remaining wheel until a man wise in the way of animals subdued the pony with a punch on its head which all but stunned it as villagers, squawking no less agitatedly than the birds in the trees, came running to enjoy the unexpected spectacle, telling each other how near they had come to death and wondering without any great concern what had become of the Oul' Wan from the big house while some wondered if the pony should be put down and who should be sent for to do it.

Outside the widow Mangan's cottage Lavinia Aylmer was breathing her last in the mud and dirt of the lane with a seemingly demented woman keening and swaying over her. By the time a couple of men came hurrying up the road to discover the actual scene of the accident Lavina Aylmer was dead.

Father Gilligan fortified himself with a couple of stiff whiskies before setting off to do his Christian duty as he saw it although he knew full well that if he shirked it no one would think any the worse of him but himself.

This would never have been a job for the curate even if O'Reilly had not taken himself off on Retreat to Rathfarnham where he might find other young priests to rejoice with him in England's downfall and maybe persuade them to his own view that such churchmen as had tacitly condoned British rule had no worthwhile part to play in the making of a newer and a better Ireland. And that was nothing as vulgar as ambition because Father O'Reilly truly believed what he preached and would always willingly take second or third place to any man of the cloth who was unswervingly dedicated to the cause of a free, united and wholly Catholic Ireland.

As he wheeled his old bicycle round the side of the Presbytery Father Gilligan wondered what he was going to say to the poor man when he saw him, for his own heart was heavy with guilt or a crime which he did not commit but for which he found himself in some way obscurely responsible. Pedalling slowly down the street he acknowledged without actually seeing the salutations of his watching parishioners who wondered among themselves where Father Peter could be going at this time of day when all the excitement had already died down with the old lady taken back to the big house and crazy Lizzie Mangan wandering aimlessly through the countryside looking for her lost baby boy. At the site of the tragedy he forced himself to look at the cottage, a bit surprised to see that it appeared no different than it always had been except that there was something dead about it as if no one had lived there for a long time. Then past the lodge where old Mrs Whitmore still kept her apprehensive watch and wondered what ill it could portend when she saw the black clad figure standing on his pedals as he laboured up the rising drive, for never a Roman priest had passed through these gates during her lifetime.

'There's a priest at the door' announced Maggie Watkins severely as if the man outside had horns and a tail.

Rory exchanged glances with a still distraught Constance and said 'Well bring him in' as he wondered what business one of them could have with him. Probably something to do with young Mangan, he thought, so he would have to see the man however badly he was feeling himself. Uncle Reggie had always said the priests were the witch doctors of the tribe and it was possible he had been sent to ask for something in the way of compensation, but anything like that would have to be left to the solicitors or the courts if it came to that. Certainly he had no intention of buying absolution for a murder which had originally been aimed at himself even if it offered the easy way out. The tragic death of his own mother whose body was at this very moment laid on the too-big bed in her room awaiting the arrival of the undertakers had to some degree hardened his heart against Gorteen and all in it although he felt that he was not being quite fair, for what had happened at the widow Mangan's was nothing less than the most rotten luck for which no one could honestly be held to blame. As voices sounded outside, Maggie Watkins' politely hostile and the priest's heavy with the rough accents of the farm, he nodded to Constance that he wished to meet the man alone and she left the room, her face streaked with disfiguring tears which only made her seem the more beautiful in his sight.

The priest stood ill at ease just inside the door, a slightly absurd figure in rusty black with bicycle clips about his skinny ankles and nervously twisting a black hat in his hands as if it was somehow giving him support. About the man was something which reminded Rory vaguely of his own mother and even the old Admiral, something which he recognised as the frailty of age and the common realisation of all three that their race was nearly run, ambition and hope equally dead within them. In spite of his own feelings Rory found himself somehow in sympathy with the man who was not himself to blame for whatever chill duty brought him into this house of mourning. 'Come in, padre' he said. 'Take a chair' and as he offered his hand he found it enclosed in a hand as soft and yielding as any woman's'. Quite irrelevantly he thought that Scrase-Green's hand had not been like that. For the Rector had been a very active man, riding to hounds and as good a shot as any in the field and he had not been above chopping his own firewood. The Romans, he thought, must have a much easier life of it and he looked to the priest to say whatever it was he had come all this way to say.

'Well, padre?' he asked as the silence between them lengthened.

'Well, Mister Aylmer - or is it Captain?' the priest began and Rory told him it was Mister, that his captaincy belonged to the war and that the war was over now.

'It's like this' recommenced Father Gilligan wondering what had happened to the soothing words which had come so easily to him over the whiskey in the Presbytery and which he had been rehearsing every turn of the wheels all the way from the village to the great house of Ardnagoilte. Faced with the set features of what he could only think of as the richest man in the village the words were lost and his throat dry as if he was saying his first Mass ever.

Rory still looked at the priest impassively. 'Yes' he asked in a carefully neutral tone. 'You have something to say to me?'

The priest swallowed and started all over again while Rory wondered where he had come from for his was not the flat accent of Wicklow but something which had in it a suggestion of wild winds and soft airs. He would be from somewhere in the West, he thought. Connemara or somewhere like that.

'It's about poor Mrs Aylmer' the priest stammered. 'I've come on behalf of the village to offer our deepest sympathy for Mrs Aylmer was very highly thought of among the people. All the Aylmers are, in fact, and sure Gorteen was blessed with all the good work your family done in the parish.'

Rory sat bolt upright. The Aylmers well thought of in Gorteen!

That was the very last thing he expected ever to hear from a Holy Roman. But if the man spoke truth it was no less than their due for all the village lived in some way on their bounty and there was never a public subscription for any cause when an Aylmer's name did not head the list. 'Paying the Danegeld' he remembered his father calling it, but brusquely and as if he would have been offended not to have been asked. And his mother had always been meticulous in caring for the tenants as far as she judged she could without actually spoiling them. But it had never occurred to anyone at Ardnagoilte that their efforts were in any way appreciated.

'Yes' continued the priest, emboldened now that he had taken the first hurdle and very well aware that he was lying in what he thought was a good cause. 'Her ladyship was very highly thought of in the village and there isn't a soul in Gorteen who does not feel for you in your very sad bereavement.'

Threatened with an unexpected display of emotion Rory said 'Sit down, padre. You'll take a peg?' and seeing the priest's bewilderment he explained 'A drink. A glass of whiskey. Peg is an army expression.'

'Oh I couldn't do that' the priest protested. Then thinking it might not be polite to refuse a drink with the man he added 'Well maybe a little one, just to drink the health of the deceased' and Rory saw nothing incongruous in his choice of words for it was an expression well known to him.

'This is very fine whiskey' said the priest appreciatively as he sipped from the cut glass tumbler. 'What would it be, if it's not too bold to ask?'

'Glen Grant' Rory told him, finding something rather appealing in the little man who had plainly forced himself to come here to pay his respects to the broken body in the room above with the window which looked over Knocknagowna to the Sugarloaf on the edge of Bray beyond.

'I'm a Bushmills man meself' said the priest, finding himself to be more comfortable in a chair and with a glass in his hand. 'I've never had Scotch whiskey before. It's very pleasant. But it wouldn't do for a priest to drink anything but Irish. And it's

146

very good too. Irish whiskey I mean. Especially Bushmills. It's a softer drink like.'

'You'll have another?' Rory asked, reaching across to take the priest's glass from his hand. 'I'm going to anyway and it's devilish miserable drinking on one's own. Oh, I forgot. Do you take water or soda?'

'Sure what can water do but spoil the taste' asked the priest almost jovially for he had already had three days drinking in a matter of hours and this young gentleman was treating him very civil indeed considering the sad circumstances that was in it. It was almost as if the two men were reaching out to each other but not daring to touch like new-met lovers. Another time and another place they would have been intuitive friends and what now stood between them and friendship was almost everything that mattered in an Irish village. Rory felt himself warming to the ingenuous little man as he poured him a bumper and lifted his own glass with a muttered 'Slainthe!'

'Slainthe go leir' responded the priest, 'Sure I didn't expect yourself to have the Irish.'

'It's little enough I have' answered Rory, easily slipping into the vernacular of his boyhood. 'Slainthe. Beannacht leat. And Go raib maith agat is about all the Irish I have in my head.'

'What more could any man need?' cried the priest delightedly. 'Sure you could travel the length and the breadth of Ireland on those three phrases alone, for the ones who understand them will talk so much Irish back at you that you won't get another word in and the ones who don't know will keep their mouths shut to cover their ignorance. If it isn't too forward a question I'd like to ask how you came by your knowledge of the Irish, for there isn't too many speaks it in these parts although it was the tongue of my own boyhood home.'

'France' Rory answered with a lopsided grin. 'British officers of all things, what I have heard called English officers in the village although most of the ones I met were Scots or Welsh if they were not downright bog Irish. They knew more of the language than I ever will. And they were better men that I shall ever be' remembering the youthful bodies bloated and discoloured and the strong young teeth bared in the rictus of death after the yellow cloud drifted over the battlefield. But that was when you knew who your enemy was, he thought. In France you would never have to look at a mild little clergyman and wonder if he had a pistol in his pocket to shoot you with. War on the shell-scarred fields of Flanders had never been as bad as this silent war among the gentle hills of his native land. 'I beg your pardon' he said to the priest.

'I said I suppose you'll be laying her ladyship to rest in Saint Luke's' repeated Father Gilligan and Rory told him not, that they would be taking the body to Waterford to be interred among her own family.

'She was a Beresford, you know' he explained and the little priest's eyes opened wide. Even in these times when all decency seemed to have been forgotten it was still something to be a Beresford of Waterford.

'Try not to feel too badly about poor old Mrs Mangan' urged the priest. 'Sure the poor woman was not in her proper senses, what with losing the boy and that. Sure she didn't know what she was doing and Mrs Aylmer one of the best friends she ever had, any of us ever had if it comes to that. Sure I've heard Mrs Mangan meself saying she'd lay down her life for Mrs Aylmer that's been so good to her.' Which was not quite true: what the widow had said in a fit of temper over her thatch was that she would swing for the old bitch but death produces its own kindly censorship and kindness to the bereaved is among the cardinal acts of charity.

'Oh no one blames Mrs Mangan as far as I know' Rory assured him. 'God knows the poor woman has suffered enough without us wanting to add to her troubles. It was an accident pure and simple. It could have happened anywhere and at anytime. If you see Mrs Mangan please tell her from me that she is always welcome at Ardnagoilte and if there is anything we can do to help she has only to ask.'

'There. That's what I mean' beamed Father Gilligan. 'The true spirit of the big house. Always a helping hand in times of trouble. Sure Gorteen is blessed with the Aylmer family. Always has been. Always will be, please God. Thank you kindly' as Rory pushed the decanter across the table silently for between the two of them words were no longer necessary. 'Would you mind if I lit me old pipe? Somehow it makes a drink more enjoyable I find.'

When both of them were companionable blowing clouds of tobacco smoke all over each other the priest sighed contentedly and said 'Ah this is very pleasant to be sure. And it's a nice house you have here, Mister Aylmer. Would you believe me if I told you this is the first time in more than thirty years I've passed through your gateway although I've wanted to often enough. I was always curious about what the big house might be like but I never got beyond your lodge in all the time I've been in Gorteen.'

'Our fault' said Rory politely. 'If we had been wiser people you would have been invited.'

'Ah well' said the priest indulgently as the whiskey worked its soothing magic within him. 'It's not all that important now. Besides I'm not sure I would have come if I'd been asked. The people, you know. They might not have understood. But that's all in the past now, thank God. We're all less wary of each other than we used to be and the country will be all the better for it. Plenty to read here' as he peered around the booklined walls. 'This would be what you call the library, I expect.'

'Yes' Rory answered. 'My father's. He was a great man for reading. These are mine' pointing to a pile of books on a low table by the fireplace. 'I wanted to learn something about Ireland.'

'Did you now?' asked the priest delightedly. 'Mind if I look?' and he reached across to pick some books at random. 'I see you've got Lecky and MacNeil and Kuno Meyer. Were they are help?'

'Not a lot' said Rory. 'All very interesting but not very illuminating. I wanted a dispassionate view but that seems to be something that does not exist. To tell you the truth, padre, what I really wanted was to find where we fit in, my own people I mean, the Anglo Irish. Do you know it never occurred to me that I was anything but Irish until I came back from the war. Now I don't know what I am.'

The priest pursed his lips and remained silent. These were very deep waters indeed for a simple man like himself to be venturing into. He picked up another book, smaller and slimmer than the rest. 'Well, wonders will never cease' he exclaimed. 'Is this really Glenanaar I'm holding in me hand? And how did you like that? Did it help in any way? It was written by a Catholic priest, but of course you would know that.'

Rory said 'Not a lot but I enjoyed it. It was a very good read. I asked Easons to send me the sort of books I would have read if I had been at the village school and that was among them. It was helpful in as far as it showed me how my own mind might have been formed if I was an ordinary Gorteen lad. The history book helped me too for I knew absolutely nothing about Irish history. There was not one word about Waterloo or the Armada in it, but then my own history book never mentioned Red Hugh O'Donnell or Brian Boru. To my mind both books seem slanted.'

'Ah well' said Father Gilligan easily. 'That's the way things are in this world. I've a few books of me own you might like a lend of. I could send someone up with them if you like.'

'That would be very kind' said Rory as he pushed the decanter across the table again and priest reached for it as naturally as if he was in his own house. This was turning out to be the most pleasant evening of his uneventful life, sitting at ease in a booklined study with a fellow booklover among trailing clouds of fragrant smoke and just chatting of this and that as easy as you like. He had quite forgotten the corpse in the room upstairs which was the real reason for his being here. 'Well just a little one' he said with the tolerant smile of the half inebriated on his innocent face. 'Then I will have to be going. Father O'Reilly is away on Retreat and there might be a sick call. But thank you very much for your hospitality and I hope I'll have the opportunity of returning it some day soon. Slainthe!'

'Slainthe yourself' rejoined Rory, rising from the deep embrace of the soft leather armchair which threatened to hold him prisoner for life. 'I'll walk you to the gate' which would be far enough not to embarrass the good old man in the sight of his parishioners. 'The gravel is very treacherous under the trees and the old dog likes me to take her out last thing' and he gave a short whistle which brought old Sheila bounding like a puppy from her private lair behind the big settee.

When he returned to the house Constance said 'What was that strange noise?' and he surprised himself by laughing as he explained 'That was Father Gilligan trying to sing 'The Rising of The Moon'. Ernie Crawford used to sing it in France, a right rebel was Ernie. Most of us were when we were with Englishmen. No one would ever have recognised it the way Father Gilligan sang it. I only hope he manages the rest of the journey home safely.'

He held her at arms length and looked closely into her face. 'Are you all right, Constance?' he asked and there was a softness in his voice which somehow filled her heart and caused it to beat faster. 'You have had a very bad time of it. Perhaps you should go away for a while. I can manage what has to be done here.'

'That would not help' she answered listlessly. Then 'Rory, I'm terribly sorry about your Mother. You must be feeling awful', laying her hand on his arm and finding it unresponsive to her touch which was not to be wondered at in the circumstances. And anyway he had never given her any sign of caring for her so it was her own foolish fault if she made dreams out of nothing more than desire, as if life could ever be as simple as that.

'I don't know' he mused. 'Somehow I don't think she would have minded all that much. She was very old and all her friends had gone before her, all the people she knew in the good old days. Uncle Reggie was the last of them and she was out of sorts with the times. And of course she never really got over Andrew's death. I was a very poor substitute for Andrew, I'm afraid.'

'I find it very hard to remember Andrew myself' said

151

Constance as if the thought had just occurred to her. 'We had such a short time together and that was all excitement so we never really got to know each other, we never lived together day by day the way I have with you. Do you know, I have not the slightest idea what Andrew was really like, what he liked to eat or what he thought about anything. I never really knew him as I know you. I can tell in an instant when anything is worrying you and...' Her voice trailed away into nothing and she felt embarrassed as if she had stripped herself naked before him without him even noticing it. It was not at all a nice feeling to have.

'You should be getting to bed' he said with a smile which could have meant anything from concern to affection. 'Tomorrow will be a very long day. I'll keep watch.'

'We'll keep watch together' she answered. And so they did, sitting silently throughout the long night hours as if they were a couple of superstitious peasants waking their dead in a mud cottage a hundred years ago while the mourning wind sighed through the ash grove. And if they had been peasants they would have heard the banshee calling from the depths of the wood.

TEN

When Lavinia Aylmer's funeral cortege passed through the Main Street of Gorteen on its way to Curraghmore of the Beresfords, every shop blind was drawn as a mark of respect for a very great lady. But when the last of the cars had breasted the rise leading to Gortmore and the South the blinds went up with a whirr and conversations became animated and even acrimonious on the subject of the Treaty which was being torn to pieces by dissenting factions in the new parliament which they would have to get used to calling Dáil Eireann.

The majority thought it a good thing because if offered peace and an end to fear but some opposed it vehemently as a betrayal of the Republic for which sixteen good men had faced a British execution squad in grim Kilmainham Jail in 1916. A few wondered uneasily how the country would survive when the practised hand of Anglo-Irishry relinquished the reins of power and told each other not to expect much from a bunch of fellas from the bogs with no experience behind them to master the complexities of running a country which had not governed itself for centuries. Others, hard and calculating men wise in the ways of their generation, looked to the bonanza of the great estates and plotted to recover lands which had never been truly theirs.

The ever pragmatic British found specious reasons for jettisoning their most loyal friends for the sake of expediency. In Gorteen it made little difference. The village still lived in the shadow of the big house but the old subserviency was gone never to return even though the euphoria of freedom was shortlived with the outbreak of a civil war over nothing more than a form of words: for the whole sorry business hinged on whether the new parliament should swear its allegiance to its own Constitution or to the King-emperor in London.

It seemed hardly enough to go to war for, especially when one war was just finished. But such things are important in Ireland and go to war they did, and with each other more bitterly than when the enemy came from another country.

Brother's hand was raised against brother and father's against son in a futile bloodletting which was all the more vicious for being fought within a closeknit community few of whom had ever been exposed to influences from beyond the borders of their own parishes. Unlike the actual war for Independence which had been fought mainly in the streets and lanes of Dublin this newer conflict spread like a cancer throughout the land between the green uniformed soldiers of Collins' National Army and the ununiformed diehards of Lynch's revivified IRA who allegiance was to the Republic as personified in the sombre figure of Eamonn de Valera who, as the only surviving leader of the 1916 Rebellion, was honoured by men on both sides but understood by none. At his bidding the unique horrors of civil war were loosed on the land to demonstrate beyond all doubt that the English held no patent on brutality and that what a Black and Tan could do well a native-born Irishman could do that much better.

It was a time for settling old scores and jockeying for position. Already the cynical game of politics had begun and some of its basest practitioners had been among the most noble when they freely offered their lives on the altar of freedom. But that was when they were poor men. Now heady with power and dazzled by the prospects of riches they constituted themselves as the new aristocracy, taking to themselves the privileges and functions of the old aristocracy without the inherent sense of propriety which had so bedevilled the old order. Now was the disputed field possessed and the spurned sister avenged. Long-buried grievances were exhumed and redressed by the power of a gun. It was a time for savage retribution.

For the Ascendancy in Ireland the bell was tolling. In Ardnagoilte, Rory heard it with an apprehension which he was scarcely able to believe.

'There's no sign of Nolan yet' he remarked to Constance over the breakfast table. 'I hope he is all right. I hope they are not going to find his body in a ditch somewhere with one of those 'Traitors and Informers Beware' notices pinned to his chest.

He was a very good man and it would be a great shame if anything happened to him on account of his devotion to the family. But I'm afraid if he does not turn up soon I'll have to do something about replacing him. Nolan was the only one who could keep the outdoor staff in order. Now I could cry to see the neglect everywhere I go and it's not much good my talking to them, they just say 'Yes, Misther Aylmer' and carry on in their own sweet way as if I was some kind of idiot boy. It surprises me now to realise how necessary Nolan was to Ardnagoilte. Without him in charge everything seems to be going to rack and ruin. The barley is still unharvested and I'm not even sure the cows are being milked regularly. Certainly the yield records are not being kept so apart from what I can see with my own eyes I have no idea at all how things are.'

He passed his huge teacup across for a refill and asked 'Do you know if his family are still in the village? Nolan thought the world of his family and he would not have gone anywhere without telling them. Perhaps they know where he is.'

'Scoiles tells me he was speaking to Mrs Nolan only a few days ago' Constance told him. He was not over Lavinia yet, not by a long chalk. She could see that in the deadness of his eyes and the abrupt way he spoke to her. Maybe it would be better for all concerned if she did go back to Roscommon, but someone had to look after him and she did not want that to be anyone other than herself. 'Scoiles says she looked well enough but he didn't like to ask her direct about Nolan. The Irish don't very much like asking anyone directly about anything, it doesn't seem mannerly to them.' She thought that she herself would have to do something soon for tongues would wag if she remained here unchaperoned. But what could she do? Someone had to see he ate his meals properly and had a clean shirt to put on, and without someone to listen to his troubles he would retreat into himself and become nothing at all like the Rory who was closer to her than a brother. With her teacup raised halfway to her lips she stopped, almost shocked to think that maybe this was what was meant by being in love for she had no idea what that might be like. Certainly she did not want to share her breakfast with any other man and it would mortify her if some other woman presided at this table. Altogether it was a very disturbing thought.

'Well, of course it would not be mannerly' he said. 'Not in ordinary circumstances. But when your head man goes missing for a matter of weeks surely one is entitled to ask what has become of him. I see that Collins is dead. According to the paper he was shot in an ambush somewhere in Cork. At least that is something they can't blame us for and I can't really say I'm all that sorry. Griffith was different. Griffith was a very good man, you can see that in every word he wrote. What Arthur Griffith wanted was the old Ireland ruled by Irishmen and who could blame him for that. But Collins and his gang, what they wanted was bloody revolution and to drive us out. I had no idea they hated us so much. We have never done them any harm.'

Constance kept her thoughts to herself. A short time ago she had privately worried that Rory showed every sign of what the dear old Admiral would have called 'going native'. All those books on Irish history and his too-openly expressed contempt for what he called the jacks-in-office at Dublin Castle. She knew instinctively that the only safe way of living in this country was to be inalterably on one side or the other for there was no middle ground. But poor Rory, in his almost childish innocence, seemed to believe that it needed no more than goodwill to bridge the gap between the two cultures when any sensible person could see at a glance that the gap was too wide and too long established for anyone ever to throw a bridge across it.

That, she thought, would be the English side of the Aylmers, the side which believed in playing a straight bat and keeping a stiff upper lip and all the other nonsense they were taught at public schools. The Irish, the more realistic side, would have known different and not wasted time and effort on a people who would despise you for liking them. It would be a very sad thing to have to leave Ireland for she had a great love for the country but it seemed to be inevitable the way things were going now and as far as she was concerned it would be much better done sooner than later. A bumble bee buzzed busily around the honeysuckle outside the window and the soft green of the fields led her eye up to the conical top of Knocknagowna. Dear Knocknagowna. The Hill of the Goats the Rector said it meant as he also said that Ardnagoilte meant the Height of the Woods and that it certainly was with woodlands stretching down on every side. A dear man, the Rector. A very dear man who knew a lot more than he ever pretended to. She just hoped they were happy now although she suspected he would miss Gorteen as long as he lived. It was strange that his tragedy was exactly the same as poor Mrs Mangan's...

Rory cut in on her thoughts as if she had spoken them aloud. 'I think I'll look in on Mrs Mangan today' he said. 'Tell her she is welcome to come back if she wishes to. After all, she was not really to blame.'

'I do not think that would be a very wise thing' she said doubtfully. 'Much better if Cook just tells that girl of hers and then she can come back if she wishes without embarrassment on either side. And if she does not wish to come back I don't mind doing the washing. Really I don't. It would be much better than just sitting around wishing I had something to do.'

He thought as if you don't do enough already. God knows what the house would be like without you to keep it in order. He said 'You are a good girl, Constance' and as she felt a flush rising from her throat to redden her cheeks she wished she could grow out of the childish habit.

At that moment the peace of the morning was destroyed by the noise of banging on the front door and of voices raised although it was not possible to understand what they were saying. Rory and Constance exchanged puzzled glances as Nellie Walker burst into the room wearing her morning blue and mob cap and with a feather duster twitching in her hand, agitated and trembling as he had never seen her before and gasping 'Mister Rory. Mister Rory. There's sojers at the door. They're askin' for you' and looking hopefully to Constance as if she alone could guarantee their safety.

Rory said 'Soldiers? Surely not.! The last of the army left

Ireland over a week ago.' As indeed they had, marching behind their bands to Westland Row station through streets lined with people cheering as if they were truly sorry to see them go, the khaki men ramrod straight and with every button gleaming to make this last parade their best ever. Dropping his napkin on the table Rory hurried into the hall followed by a white-faced Constance determined that no harm should come to him if she could possibly avert it.

Soldiers they were. But not in khaki. In the doorway stood Derry Keogh flush-faced and arrogant in a uniform of drab green with his tunic collar hanging open about his bull-like neck and an officers' Sam Browne belt slanting across his chest. A holster was strapped to his right knee and in his hand was a big black revolver which he waved menacingly as Rory approached and said uncertainly 'Good morning, Keogh.' Behind Keogh he could see about ten other men dressed in the same shade of green and carrying rifles with bayonets glinting in the morning sun. Among them was a leering Nolan with the three bars of a sergeant on his arm.

'Captain Keogh ta you!' snapped the onetime Derry. 'An' if ya know what's good fer ya y'll remember that. We're looking fer Childers. He's here somewhere with David Robinson. Ya can save yerself a lotta trouble be just handin' him over. There's a price on his head.'

'Childers?' asked Rory, mystified. 'But he is one of the best friends you have.'

Keogh scowled. 'Never was an Englishmen yet was a friend ta Ireland. Centuries we've suffered under you an' yer like but the boot's on the other foot now.' He peered beyond Rory to where Scoiles and Maggie Watkins stood halfway up the stairs trying not to draw attention to themselves. 'We've got our countery back agen!' he roared in his excitement 'an' if yer lot wantsta go on livin' here y'll haveta stop lookin' down yer noses at us an' show us proper respect. If it was only upta me I'd put the whole lotta yez up agen the wall an' I'd enjoy it. Now fer the last time where is Childers? We'll get him wan way or another so the sooner ya hand him over the better it'll be fer you.'

Rory noticed that Nolan had taken himself off round the side of the house, to search the stables he supposed. But he would find no one there who ought not to have been there. Maybe he just wanted his old workmates to see him in his grand uniform. 'I don't even know Mister Childers' he answered, trying very hard to keep his temper under control for it would not help anyone if he gave way to the outrage within him and telling himself that times had changed, so he would have to change with them.

'Don'tcha?' barked Keogh, 'Well she does' waving his revolver in Constance's direction while the soldier in Rory noticed that the safety catch was off and wondered if Keogh knew about that. It was the commonest error among people not used to firearms. 'Accordin' ta my information she's a cousin of his.'

'I am' she admitted. 'But how close I cannot say. To my knowledge the last time I saw Erskine Childers was over five years ago.' Some built-in caution warned her not to use the words 'Dublin Castle' for to these people that would mean she was a spy since everyone with an admitted British connection was a spy in their eyes and whether there was anything to spy about was not of any consequence.

'You're his cousin' repeated Keogh, his eyes darting about the hallway and his finger tightening on the trigger as if he himself might be attacked at any moment.

As casually as he could with his temper boiling in him Rory said 'Well perhaps you had better search the house if you won't take my word for it. But I repeat that I have never seen Mister Childers in my life' and he stood aside from the door.

'I mean to' said Keogh, waving his men into the hall where they scattered through the downstairs rooms, looking as if they would have liked to apologise but not daring to. 'And if I find as much as wan shotgun cartridge, let alone any firearms, in this house you'll have told yer last lie. Go on!' to his hesitant soldiers. 'Every room an' everything in every room. You keep an eye on these two, sergeant, an' don't hesitate to shoot if they make a move.' For Nolan had now rejoined the party and was standing with his rifle pointed at Rory's chest as if nothing could give him greater pleasure than to pull the trigger.

'We worried about you, Nolan' began Rory, only to be told that it was Sergeant Nolan and not to forget it. 'We thought maybe you were ill.'

'Did ya now?' asked Nolan, grinning as if at some secret joke. 'Now wasn't that kind've yer honour, ta be worryin' yer head over the likes've a common oul' farm labourer. 'Tis little ya worried when I wuz doin' the work of two men for a boy's pay. Then it was 'Nolan this' an' 'Nolan that' as if I hadn't a name've me own an if y'd tried ta call me Mister Nolan sure it would have stuck in yer throat so it would. I mind last year when I asked ya ta make me money up an' ya said y'd think about it an' then never did nothin' expectin' us ta be grateful for a few cansa milk anna few bagsa podadas when you were livin' like lords up here, with mate every day've the week an' us scrapin' a livin' any way we can in the village.

'Fifteen years I've worked on this place, kapein' you an' yours in the lappa luxury with wine an' cigars an' all yer orders with never a thought how we were livin' ourselves an' us like strangers in our own land.' He lifted the sagging rifle and continued bitterly 'If ya wanta do me a favour now, Misther Aylmer, just make wan false move, just was false move is all I ask, so's I can plug ya where ya stand same's I plugged the bloody oul' Admiral. An' her with ya, her that thinks Gorteen's muck under her feet an' can't give a man the timea day when she passes him in the village an' everywan lookin' at him like he wuz an eejit or somethin'. Just wan false move an' y'll make me the happiest man in Wickla taday.'

For a chill moment it seemed that Nolan was going to pull the trigger anyway, but Keogh came clattering down the stairs as his men returned from their searching with nothing to report. 'Have ya seen the lavatery, boys?' he asked in high glee. 'Sure yev never seen the like've it in yer life. All nice soft paper fer their nice soft bums, nonea last week's Independent for them. An' every bed has two sheets on it. Sure y'd betther all come up an' take a look for y'll never see the likes've it agen. Sure even the Holy Father hisself doesn't live half as well as the Aylmers of Ardnagoilte. Go on up, lads, but be very careful notta touch anythin' with yer dirty labourin' hands.' As the men unwillingly climbed the stairs he added conversationally 'Sure I wouldn'ta believed it if I didn't see it with me own two eyes. It's no wonder ya don't wanta leave Ireland for their isn't another race'd put up withya anywhere in the whole wide world' and he spat into the fireplace in disgust while Rory thought If I was half the man my father was I'd tackle the pair of them and chance being shot. But there was Constance to consider.

In time these fledgling soldiers of the Irish National Army in their creased new uniforms and caps with sunburst badges inscribed in Gaelic 'For the Glory of God and the Honour of Ireland' clattered noisily out of the house and disappeared down the drive in an ex-British army lorry to wherever their next assignment might be. 'Wouldya like a cuppa tay, Miss Constance?' asked Maggie Watkins to whom tea was the sovereign remedy for all human ills. 'The kettle's just on the boil' for the big black kettle at the side of the stove was always on the boil and Maggie herself had a great need for a soothing cup of tea with a couple of aspirins to help settle her nerves.

'That would be very nice' agreed Constance. As Maggie left the room she said to Rory 'What an unpleasant business. Have you ever known anyone as disloyal as Nolan? I don't even know what he is talking about me passing him in the street. It must have been when I first came here and didn't know the staff very well. But it tells you the whole story. Much better if we all get out while we can, Rory. Things here can only get worse. Everyone who can afford it is getting out.'

'I'll not be turned off my own land' he said doggedly, and now she could see something of Lavinia in him. 'And I won't be chased out of Ireland either. Here I was born and here I will die, God willing. The Dáil, as they call it, is committed to preserving law and order all over the country. These are just local bullyboys working off old scores while they can. Once the new government settles down things will be just as they were. Some very sound men in the new government. Cosgrave is a business man and O'Higgins is very strong on law and order. When they get this civil war sorted out life will be just the same as it always was. After all they need us for stability. None of them has any experience of government or anything else for that matter. So they will have to keep the permanent officials on, then there's the Civil Service and the Customs and the Police and if the landowners go half the country will be out of work. As I see it we are just going through a bad patch and when we are through everything will settle down the way it always was. Once order is restored Keogh and his like will be put in their proper places again. I think they will have to call in men like Powerscourt and Holmpatrick, men the people know and respect to get themselves off on the right foot. Glenavy maybe, the people know and like him too. Or Ashburn, though he is as bolshie as the worst of them.'

'The facts speak for themselves. Whatever may or may not have been decided in London the Irish have no administrators, won't have for years yet. In the meantime it's up to us to do our part for it's our country too. There were Aylmers in Ireland before America became a nation. As a matter of fact there were Aylmers there too, one of them was killed at Vicksburg. And as far as I am concerned there will be an Aylmer at Ardnagoilte as long as breath is left in me.' He stopped, surprised at himself for actually speaking what had been in his mind for longer than even he realised. For this was Aylmer land, passed down through the generations into his keeping and he was determined not to fail in his trust. But it seemed very bad form actually to say to out loud.

Constance held her peace, herself surprised to uncover such depths of emotion in what was normally a placid man and thinking how strangely stubborn men could be when their pride was involved. For good or ill she was determined to remain here with him if that was what he wanted to do though it was difficult to imagine any good coming of it. Almost certainly the land would be confiscated on some pretext or other, she could remember her own father predicting that if ever Westminster conceded Home Rule and what was happening now went much further than that. At best they would be taxed out of existence and at worst they would live every day of their lives in fear of the gunman behind the hedge or the hooded bands maiming inoffensive cattle by night as they had in her grandfather's day. The only sensible way to go was out, but with Rory in his present mood there was no point in repeating that. One look at the set face which appeared English to the Irish and Irish to the English was enough to tell her how futile further argument would be. There was something in Rory which had not been in Andrew, something rocklike which Andrew had not needed because no one had ever disputed his right to be the master or Ardnagoilte. And what a short time ago that seemed to be. Ireland had changed since 1916 as the rest of the world had changed since 1914 and they were all going to find adjustment difficult if not impossible. Fervently she prayed that Rory would not do anything to provoke trouble but in his present mood it was not worth while counselling caution since he would never admit there was anything to be cautious about.

'It seems to me' she began haltingly, not sure what she wanted to say but knowing that something had to be said to break the silence which hung between them as a wall. 'It seems to me...'

'Yes?' The tone was polite enough. Too polite in fact for the face was still set and unyielding. Her heart sank.

Then there was a scuffling, stumbling sound in the hall and panting sobs which echoed in the quiet house. The door was pushed open and Nellie Walker came staggering into the room clutching her green outdoor apron, eyes wild and mouthing incomprehensibly, shaking from head to foot with fear. 'Misthur Rory!' she moaned, looking at him as if he alone could take the fear away. 'Misthur Rory. The stables. In the stables...'

Now it begins, thought Rory, they've done something to the horses, as Nellie mumbled something about being out gathering the eggs when she found it. Whatever 'it' was she could not force herself to say.

'Take care of her' he ordered and for a moment Constance had a surprised glimpse of the infantry officer he had once been. Before she could answer he was out of the door and running past the window to the stables, his heart sick with a premonition as he remembered the secret knowledge in Nolan's leering face.

As he came around the corner of the house towards the stables he breathed a prayer of thanks to see old Sheila snoozing contentedly in her own little suntrap in the angle of the open door. Then fear came on him again when the dog lay still at his approach when normally she would be lurching towards him now with her tail awag and eager to be off to wherever they might be going together.

'Sheila! Sheila!' he called when his whistle of command failed to rouse the sleeping dog and he told himself that it just could not be, that the old bitch was sickening for something. But as he came closer he saw the insert body with its golden pelt lifeless as a fur rug and the blood matting dark red around half a dozen stab wounds and was sick in his soul. Great sobs hurt his chest as he knelt to embrace the slain animal and his tears fell in torrents on her savaged head to mix with the caking blood. For there is no sorrow known to man greater than losing a dog, no greater bond than the mystical link which is so natural as to be unnoticed.

'The evil bastard!' he screamed. 'The dirty rotten coward!' For she would have no fear of Nolan, the man who used to tickle her stomach and call her 'Sheila deelish' as he played with her almost every day. She would have no fear of Nolan, her friend. Probably the last thing she did in life was to wave her bushy tail as her old friend approached stealthily with his bayonet poised to strike and strike again in a dastardly act which he knew would hurt Rory more than anything else ever could.

He bent to place his face against the old dog which had become more than a part of his life over the recent years, whimpering with affection as he approached, scampering ahead of him as they walked through meadow or wood, occasionally glancing back to be sure he was following or lying companionably across his feet as he smoked a pipe in the evening and half listened to his mother and Constance having one of those unimportant women's conversations. At such times he had thought his life to be complete for he was not an ambitious man and was well content with what he had, always with Sheila near at hand, never demanding anything but to be with him. He knew that he would miss the old dog miserably. Then he had a vision of the Judas creeping up with his poised bayonet, whispering endearments in his harsh Wicklow accent while the trusting animal looked on her assassin with affection. For man is the only animal who betrays a friend.

He could not - would not - count the wounds, but there were so many of them and every one so deep that more than killing was intended. The treacly brown eyes would have looked fondly on the slayer and the long red tongue would have been lolling happily before the first terrible stroke, and after that it would have been too late. Again a sorrow too great to be borne overcame him and the tears flowed again. When Constance came hurrying to find him he was on his knees cradling the old dog's head in his arms and crying as no man should ever be seen to cry. Too shocked to cry, Constance fell to her knees and placed her arm about Rory in what she knew was a futile gesture for he would have no thought of her or anyone else now. But it helped to be able to share his misery and then suddenly her own tears came and she cried on his shoulder until the tweed was sodden wet.

After an age Rory was cried out with no more tears to give. Rising to his feet and carrying the dead dog in his arms like a child he strode past the house and over the lawn to the drive leading to the village, Constance clutching his arm as she ran to keep up with the hurrying man, fearing that this latest tragedy could only be the forerunner of other and greater tragedies. She had never seen Rory look so resolute, so fierce. No one living ever had.

Father Gilligan heard the commotion as he was looking over his books and thinking there was not much among them likely to be of assistance to that poor Aylmer lad. The Homes of Tipperary and My New Curate were good books to be sure but there was nothing in them which might help Mister Aylmer to find the identity he was so clearly seeking. As the uproar mounted the priest moved into the big bay window overlooking the village street.

In the roadway outside Captain Keogh was drilling his men and looking the part as he kept them in the best of order, making them form two and fours and issuing commands so crisply it was hard to believe that this was the same Derry Keogh who had been a nobody just a short while ago but now was the pride of the village. For he looked like a captain and he acted like a captain so there was no limit to what he might yet achieve and who had a better right after all he had done for the old Cause.

Independence was working wonders for the country. Men never before heard of were emerging to be the new rulers of the land and the people had recovered their lost pride, for which he heartily thanked the good God who had strengthened them during their darkest days. The ability was there. It had always been there. All they had ever needed was the change to demonstrate it. It was a great pity about all the killings, young Kevin Barry and dozens more in Dublin. Even here in Gorteen which had seemed to slumber through the war there had been young Scrase-Greene, the oul' Admiral, poor Mrs Mangan's lad (and wasn't it a very strange thing that anyone should bother to shoot an omadaun of a boy? but maybe they thought they had enough reason) and that poor old man of the roads they called Shawneen. Not forgetting good Constable Madigan, the best friend Gorteen ever had for since his death there was no one to bring the papers nor collect the medicine for the poor oul' crayturs in the glens. Madigan's contemptuous killing had always weighed heavily on Father Gilligan: the man was only doing his job and he was as good a Catholic as anyone and he had deserved better of them, whoever it was.

But that the way the world turned and it seemed that every nation had to find freedom at the end of its own Via Dolorosa. While the old priest watched the drilling men the Captain called them to attention and ordered 'Present arms!' as Father O'Reilly came from the chapel where he would have been hearing children's confessions, in soutane and biretta and with his stole neatly folded in his left hand. As the rifles crashed down as good as anything the British ever managed the Curate smiled and raised his right hand in a blessing while Father Gilligan angrily told himself it was a lot of codology and that that fella'd overstep the mark one of these days. To see all his airs and graces you'd think it was Cardinal Logue hisself, so you would.

But the drill was not the cause of the noise which he had heard. The few loungers who assembled here daily to watch Captain Keogh drill his men were respectfully silent as Father O'Reilly made the sign of the cross to bless the troops and still the noise continued, even becoming louder until, from the right hand side of the window Rory Aylmer came into view clutching his pathetic little bundle and with that nice young woman from Roscommon hanging on his arm and almost running to keep up with his long, purposeful strides, left-right, left-right, left-right. A crowd of villagers followed like, the priest thought, seagulls after the plough. Again he wondered what the commotion could be about -had there been another accident of some kind? - until Rory passed close enough for Father Gilligan to see the blood-matted dog and the lifeless hang of its head and the desolation in young Aylmer's eyes, striding like a sleepwalker or a man who goes to his death on the gallows. Instantly the priest knew what must have happened and he thought Holy Mother of God, what kind of people can we be to do such a dreadful thing.

The soldiers ordered arms as if they had been doing it for years instead of mere weeks while Father O'Reilly and their Captain chatted together before the men were dismissed for the night. Then both men stopped as the small procession approached and 'Eyes front!' snapped Captain Keogh to his wavering company. To his credit not one man dated peep over his shoulder to see the cause of all the hullabaloo.

The young priest looked coldly at Rory Aylmer as he pushed his way through the line of soldiers with all that was left of old Sheila hanging limply from his arms. Again the tears forced themselves from his reddened eyes and his voice trembled as he demanded of Derry Keogh 'Tell me this, Keogh. Is this an English dog or an Irish dog. Is it a Protestant or a Catholic dog? Has it the right to...?' Then his voice really broke and he was crying like a frustrated child, pressing his face into the lifeless fur of the animal. Derry Keogh's face darkened in anger but the young priest said suavely 'Well, judging be the company it keeps I'd say it was an Ascendancy dog for any decent Irish dog wouldn't be seen in your company and the sooner the both of you is out of Gorteen the happier we all will be.'

Derry frowned at the priest, started to say something and thought better of it as he saw the smirk on the face of his sergeant. The onlookers shrieked at the wit of the priest's repartee and repeated it to each other in case it had not been heard the first time. One old woman cackled derisively 'Such a lot of fuss over an oul' dog. Sure yed think it was a Christian'd been killed' and that it was which stung old Father Gilligan as he stood on the step of his Presbytery, outraged and bewildered for never before had anyone in Gorteen dared act badly in his presence. Something snapped inside his mind as he came half running across the road to confront all of them at once and risk losing the parish of Gorteen. And he was white with temper.

Captain Keogh mumbled 'Sure I didn't know anythin' about it at all, Father'. Father Gilligan ignored him. 'Silence!' he shouted. Then 'SILENCE!' in a tone no one had ever heard him use before. So astonished were they all that they fell silent as one person while the little priest quivered with anger and his brain in such a ferment that the words would not come to his lips at first.

Then 'Father O'Reilly' he commanded, and commanded is the right word for the little man seemed visibly to grow in stature as he outfaced his Curate in the certainty that he would be obeyed. 'Father O'Reilly. Go you now into the Presbytery and wait till I come to you for there's one or two things we'd better talk about before we're both much older.' As the young Curate hesitated before stalking across the road to the priests' house, a model of offended rectitude with his still young face flushing deep red from his throat to his cheeks, Julia Begley clutched her cardigan tightly about her neck as if there might be some protection in that and muttered prayers to her special saint to help the poor man before he went too far. For he had the wild look of a man who has had enough of caution and indeed there was little of the familiar Father Gilligan in the moist face under the sparse greying hair which lifted from his forehead as if the wind was ruffling it.

There was not one villager there who could believe his eyes. All of them had seen the Parish Priest in the guise of a caring parent gently chiding them from the altar and this was not a bit like the man they were used to. If there was murmuring among them it was concern for the poor oul' fella seemed fit to bust. Rory stood by hugging his dead dog and Constance tried to comfort him with one arm about his shoulders while the soldiers remained rigidly at attention because Captain Keogh had not given them the 'Stand at Ease' and they knew better than to anticipate his orders.

Priests are not often at a loss for words. Father Gilligan coughed and thought furiously. Then he coughed again as he said in what was a very big voice for a small man 'People of Gorteen, I'm ashamed of you. I'm ashamed to be your priest for it's been wasting me time I've been all these years trying to make Christians out of a pack of savages.'

They listened in oxlike silence, amazed. One man quietly detached himself from the crowd and made his way homeward and a soldier shuffled his feet until Derry commanded 'Steady in the ranks!' Insulated by their own grief Rory and Constance stood by like bit actors, aware only that for some reason the jeering and sniggering had stopped.

Once started, Father Gilligan could not have stopped even if he wanted to. Small, frail and defiant the words poured from him in a torrent which would not be checked. 'After all me teaching and praying all the years I've ben in Gorteen ye still haven't got the slightest idea why the Great God of Heaven an' Earth and all things sent his only son, Our Lord Jesus Christ, to live amongst us and teach us God's law that first of all we have to love each other and to care for each other before we can be fit even to approach the throne of God and His Most Blessed Mother. The savages in the African jungle have more charity than can be found in the village of Gorteen today, and may God forgive us all for it. May He forgive you for persecuting a man who has never done anything but good in the parish and may He forgive me for not being a better priest.'

'Oh, no, Father, No' they protested. Their priest was a special being, standing in almost direct relationship with the Almighty and they would not have him take any blame on himself.

Father Gilligan waved away their protest and continued 'How many of you said your prayers this morning? How many of you said a little prayer to Saint Anthony for some special intention? Well I can tell you that at this very minute in heaven good Saint Anthony is crying his eyes out for what happened to a poor oul' dog that never did a thing wrong in its innocent life, which is more than can be said for most of you' which was a very shrewd thrust from the custodian of every secret in the village. 'All that poor oul' dog did was to love its master the same as we should love our Master Our Lord and Saviour Jesus Christ with all our hearts and with all our minds. And as for the coward that tried to hurt Mister Aylmer through his little dog - well, I wouldn't like to stand in his place on judgement day so I wouldn't, especially when Saint Anthony gets his hands on him.'

Somehow he was losing direction and side-tracking himself. That was happening too often nowadays for a priest should be able to see a problem from all sides. But he was so vexed. So perplexed. So... moidered was the word he was looking for. Moidered was what he was in truth and sick in his soul. With humility he thought It's too long I've been in this job entirely, far too long shut away in presbyteries and religious houses to know what people are really like in this day and age when, God help us, women went round showing their legs and smoking cigarettes (but not in Gorteen: the first hussy to show herself in the village not properly dressed would get a skelp of his stick and the biggest penance of her life) and wicked men shot innocent dogs because they didn't like their owners.

'Well, what I'm saying is that you all ought to be ashamed of yourselves acting like a lot of savages disgracing your Faith and your country like you'd never been told better' with a sidelong glance at Rory's ravaged face, for how would a simple Irish priest know that the only time an Englishman may cry openly is over the death of his dog. Captain Keogh wondered too. It disturbed him to see a grown man crying over an oul' dog and him a man who had seen war at first hand. A very strange class've a people the English were to be sure. And that gerrl of his was just as bad.

The crowd was quiet as if they were in church and the little priest's own eyes were moist when he said to Rory 'Mister Aylmer. More than anyone else I know how much this village and this country means to you and it's a sorry return you've got for it. But for sweet charity's sake don't let it turn your heart against us. For it wasn't all of Gorteen or all or Ireland. It was just one wicked man and every country has its share of those. Why God let's these things happen I don't rightly know but sometimes good really does come out of evil. So I ask you in the name of every man, woman and child here present, don't take yourself away from us, Mister Aylmer. Don't let the last of the Aylmers leave Gorteen with bad memories.'

Now there was a murmuring in the crowd for Father Gilligan was a much loved man. Still lost in his grief Rory heard it not as he had not heard one word of the priest's diatribe with his heart still chilled for love of an old dog which didn't even have a pedigree. The last thing he remembered was of walking down the road to the village with no idea at all what he was going to do when he got there. He had a confused impression of people praying around him. Then he heard the old priest whom he had hoped would become his friend telling them sternly to be off to their homes and to go on their knees asking God's forgiveness for the sin of failing in charity, reminding them that in the sight of Our Lord they were equally as bad as the Roman soldiers who had pressed the crown of thorns into his blessed head as the Saviour uncomplainingly took upon Himself the burden of all our sins. Somehow he found himself responding to the old priest's voice and believing as a child believes a fairy tale because he trusts the teller. One terrible sentence fixed itself in his mind. 'If Our Blessed Lord had been born in Gorteen you'd have crucified him just the same!' and the frisson of horror from the listening crowd while Father Gilligan called out 'You. Joe Foley! You get your trap out and drive Mister Aylmer and the lady back home. And while you're there you can help Mister Aylmer do whatever he thinks necessary for the old dog.'

Then Captain Keogh's voice, authoritative as an officer's should be. 'No, Father. Sergeant Nolan will take two men up to Ardnagoilte and see the dog's put properly to rest wherever Mister Aylmer says.' Then himself shouting angrily 'NO! She's my dog. I'll bury her myself' knowing that if he found himself alone with Nolan he would strangle the man with his bare hands even if he got himself bayoneted in the attempt.

So it was that poor old Sheila, rising twelve and with not a lot left of her natural life anyway, was laid to rest in a spot which she would have known well, a sunwarmed clearing among the rioting roses which were to have been Larry Mangan's next task when he had cleared the weeds and wrapped in a superfine khaki tunic with a row of medal ribbons on the left breast and the three embroidered stars of a captain on each cuff. There were no last words, only a tribute of scalding tears which left Rory feeling weak and ashamed until Constance took his arm and gently guided him back into the house.

Father Gilligan watched the trap moving sedately down the village street. Joe Foley had a sense of occasion and this was no time to be whipping up the oul' pony and scattering the chickens in their way for - the thought came to him unexpectedly - it was just like going to a funeral, and who ever heard of anyone having a funeral for an oul' dog. One quick glance at the faces of his two passengers decided him to keep the notion to himself for they might not think it as funny as he did. But it was funny just the same.

The priest watched the trap out of sight sick at heart that he had somehow failed the poor man who had opened his heart and his home to him. On and off since then he had thought of that unexpected meeting of minds which only the good Lord Himself could have planned and which gave him pleasure every time he remembered it. That the poor man was looking for something was very plain. What if he had been looking for a way back to the faith of his fathers? for they were all Catholic once. What if the man had been reaching out to him for support and he had failed in his sacred duty? The worst of it was that probably he would never know now for he sensed in Mister Aylmer a revulsion which would take him as far away from Gorteen as he could get and that as soon as he could manage it. That was only natural. But maybe a novena to Saint Jude would cause him to have second thoughts for the kinsman of Christ had great powers in things despaired of. A Gorteen without an Aylmer at the big house wouldn't be the same place at all, so it wouldn't.

'Thank you, Derry' he said, half raising his hand in what might have been a blessing or a salute, as Captain Keogh roared 'Present arms!' and the rifles came down crash-crash-crash in perfect unison and the officer snapped his right hand to the peak of his cap in a flat-handed salute.

'Good lads. Good lads' Father Gilligan nodded to the saluting soldiers and made his way across the street to where a worried Julia Begley waited on the presbytery steps, working her apron through her fingers and thinking they would never hear the end of this day's work. 'Of Father Pethur, Father Pethur' she wailed. 'What've ya done? What've ya done? and he answered as jauntily as if the selfsame thing was not worrying him 'What I've been wanting to do for a long time, Julia Begley. Spoke me mind out straight without fear nor favour, and it feels grand.

D'ye think y' could lay yer hands on a nice piece of steak for me tea? With maybe a few onions if there's any in the house?'

'Oh Father!' she whispered, thinking If only he wasn't a priest and me married to him it's the proudest woman in all Ireland I'd be this day. And him as cocky as you please as if he wasn't frightened near out of his life. For this would have to go further, and then who knew where it would end. Steak indeed! 'It's a fast day, Father. Saint Lawrence Deacon and Martyr, trusted friend of Pope Sextus the Second.'

'And who might he be when he's at home? asked the priest with a show of bravado. 'What's he ever done for Ireland? Answer me that. A steak is what I fancy, Julia Begley, and a steak is what I'll have for I'm going to be a martyr meself and it's hard work being a martyr on fish.' He stepped before her into the hallway for no one takes precedence over a PP in his own parish. 'And now' he said grimly. 'I'm going to wipe the floor with O'Reilly. He can run and tell the bishop that too and bad cess to him. Don't forget. Plenty of onions, Julia. And potatoes. Don't forget the potatoes.'

It was no good. All the whiskey in the world would not dull the pain or help him to sleep for he would never sleep again, he knew that as he lay in bed watching the shadow of the beech tree on his carpet in the ghostly light of the callous moon.

Because one must he had sat at table with Constance while a subdued Maggie Watkins brought soup, meat and pudding and took them away again almost untasted. Which did not surprise her in the least for it was little enough she could eat thinking of how poor Sheila had died and she the softest creature the good Lord ever made. But she was most worried about Master Rory whom she still saw as an untidy boy in short trousers forever disappearing off somewhere with that Larry Mangan and never willing to say where they had been. Now Master Andrew had been nothing like that at all. Master Andrew had always known his own position and though he would never be rude to servants (none of the old gentry was ever that) he kept everyone firmly in their place just like his old father. And may the earth lie lightly on them both.

Master Rory had always been different and many's the time she worried about that. If there was one thing certain in Ireland it was that no good ever came of people mixing outside their own class: never was and never would be. Too fond of that he had been, too fond of the likes of the Mangans and every tinker he met between here and Iveraun. But he had grown out of that foolishness, thank God, and when the time came he knew which side he was on. Not like that poor man Childers that had just been arrested in Glendalough before the eyes of his wife and no one knew what was going to happen to him. Which just went to show that a man should stick by his own kind for he would find help nowhere else. For when it comes to the point blood always tells, blood makes the decisions we think we make for ourselves. It was a great pity about Erskine Childers. But he had brought it on himself and neither side wanted him.

When Rory waved the coffee away and told her to bring the whiskey decanter she hesitated until she saw the grim set of his mouth, just like his father it was and no one ever dared argue with him. Then she thought maybe it is better that way, that though time is a great healer the bottle does it quicker and at least it would help him get through this miserable night. For some time Rory and Constance sat together staring into the log fire, each seeing a different picture and each thinking their own separate thoughts until he mumbled something about having a smoke outside and Constance knew that the little mound of newly turned earth was pulling him back and that he was best left alone with his sorrow.

In fact five minutes of it was all that he could stand, thinking of the devoted creature with all its savage wounds just a few feet below the ground, so he set off down the drive walking to anywhere at all, ears cocked hopefully for the rustle of four legs through fallen leaves or eyes gleaming golden in the dark of the night. When he thought he had walked himself tired he returned to the house and went quietly up to the room which had been his since boyhood and so familiar that he longer saw the faded floral wallpaper or the equally faded oriental carpet which he always associated with Uncle Reggie, but that could just have been imagination. On the walls were the prints of the Boyhood of Raleigh and The Last Fight of the Temeraire, a French landscape which could have been an original and a heavily bearded personage which was the regal Edward VII in all his glory. Somewhere in the clutter which he allowed no servant to touch would be the collection of birds' eggs and pieces of rock whose significance he had long forgotten. Like all other furniture in the house the bedroom furniture was massive and ageless. He could remember being made to share the big brass-knobbed bed when Andrew had had chicken pox so they would not give it to the rest of the household. Now he undressed automatically and sank into it, hoping desperately for the forgetfulness of sleep.

But sleep did not come. Sleep would never come again. And the whiskey was not helping at all, if anything it set his mind racing in a dozen different directions and all of them stupid. This is absurd, he told himself. Grieving over an old dog. He had seen men die ugly deaths on the battlefield but none had affected him except to make him grateful for his own survival. But a dog was different. All a dog asks of life is to be always in the company of one man and that man, be he purest saint or worst sinner unhung, the dog will follow faithfully until they both topple over the edge of living. I must stop this, he told himself. It is ridiculous...but. And again treacherous tears took him unawares until all that was left was a dry sobbing that hurt the back of his throat. And he vowed to never have another dog.

In a haze of sleep he fancied he heard a tap on his bedroom door, the timid kind of tap which does not really want to be heard. As he turned his head the door swung gently open as Constance came into the room, her face haggard in the moonlight but to him inexpressibly beautiful as she clutched her dressing gown beneath her chin. For a long moment they stared at each other and he knew that for them both, life at Ardnagoilte had become a dream betrayed. In a very small voice she said 'I miss Sheila too Rory.'

When Maggie Watkins served breakfast her eyes widened to see them both so curiously alive when only yesterday they had been so plunged in gloom they had not been able to eat a thing. Now here he was wanting eggs and bacon with fried bread, if you don't mind, and young Mrs Aylmer wondering if Cook could manage to give her a plain omelette. Maggie smiled to herself. A woman ought not to be a widow forever and they still had years of life before them, so may they both live long and be happy together. Maggie's step was light and she smiled knowingly as she placed the food on the table. When she had gone to the kitchen again Rory said 'Whatever can have come over Maggie? She looks years younger.'

As he pricked a lightly fried egg with his fork to send its yellow goodness spreading over the fried bread Constance murmured 'I think she guesses and I don't care. The whole world may know as far as I'm concerned. Rory, my love, are you still set on leaving Ardnagoilte?'

He waited until he had chewed his food. 'I don't see anything else for it. Last night you mentioned Scrase-Greene and that reminded me of something he once said to me. Scrase-Greene was a much wiser man than any of us ever gave him credit for. He said that all wars are fought over land, that the native Irish will always hate us because they think they should have the whole country but we believe we are entitled to the parts we have cultivated and made since our ancestors first arrived in Ireland. He was right. There will be fighting. But it will not be between armies. It will be something more difficult. Policemen shot and animals (again the treacherous tears were very close behind his eyes) murdered. Stables and barns set afire during the night and servants too frightened to stay. Like young Fogarty. Fogarty has disappeared and no one knows if he is alive or not. And all done by men you never see so you can't hit back at them. That little priest, that Father Something, is the only man in Gorteen I could trust and he could be the ringleader for all I know. The history of Ireland is full of it and

I can't see an end to it, not in our lifetime anyway. Scrase-Greene believed they actually enjoy their grievances and that may well be the top and the bottom of the whole miserable mess.'

He looked through the window to where Knocknagowna rose in a dull blue cone, a hill pretending to be a mountain and added very soberly 'No. I don't want to stay at Ardnagoilte and I could not ask you to. Sooner or later the barn would go up in the night and then we would know we were the target and I could not ask you to share that. So I'll be off to Dublin today to tell Hewitt to put the property on the market. It's hard luck on the staff but I fancy they will not be sorry to leave the place either and we shall have to do the best we can for them.' He wiped his mouth with his napkin and reached into his pocket for his pipe. 'Would you like to come with me? It might do you good to get away from here for a while, see what's new in Arnotts or Switzers while I see my man of business and maybe have a bite at the Shelbourne or Jammet's afterwards. Stay overnight if you like.'

'It is very tempting' she replied. 'But if you don't mind I would rather stay here for the present. I've become very fond of Ardnagoilte.' And, she thought, one of us should be here, just in case. 'Have you any idea where you would like to settle in England? Did you ever find out where the Aylmers came from originally?'

'Never bothered. As far as I am concerned the Aylmers always belonged to Ardnagoilte. And I'm not all that keen on settling in England. I like the English well enough but I don't think I would like to live among them. They are a very insensitive people, think that if they mistake you for an Englishman they are paying you a compliment. I remember in France once, a sergeant of the Buffs told me he would never have taken me for a Paddy. His very words, and he was talking to an officer of an Irish regiment. Same man told my chaps his lot had been sent to stiffen us up, after we had fought right through the war without anyone's help. And he just could not bring himself to call me 'Sir' or to salute properly the way he saluted an English officer. I think maybe that is what they disliked about Erskine

Childers. Did he look down his nose at them do you remember?'

Constance tried to recall a glittering occasion at Dublin Castle a lifetime ago. 'I rather fancy that he did, not only at them but at the whole world as I remember him. But they would not know that. They would think it was only at themselves because in the end everything comes back to them. To be quite honest, my dear, much as I should hate leaving Ardnagoilte I would be quite happy to leave Ireland the way things are now. Everything is too uncertain. But if not England, where? Scotland perhaps? Or Wales?'

'The colonies, I thought' he replied with a sidelong glance to see her reaction. 'Africa, perhaps, although I do not think I would like it all that much. Australia or New Zealand. From what I hear New Zealand is fine farming country and land prices are reasonable. If we get a half decent price for Ardnagoilte we ought to be able to make a good start in New Zealand. Decent climate and they are speak English. We should stand a good chance of making a go of it there.' The line of his jaw tautened and his eyes narrow to slits. 'One thing I am quite certain of is that I don't want to go on living in a country where they murder dogs.'

ELEVEN

The bleakness of a November evening was all over the land and it lay like a pall on the usually pretty harbour of Kingstown which was now called by its ancient name of Dun Laoghaire or the Fort of King Leary. For since the British had retreated to their mainland stronghold a frenzy of decolonisation had occurred. Streets were renamed to honour local patriots and the street signs were in Gaelic and English, with Gaelic in first place. Customs Officers wore the badge of Brian Boru's harp on their caps and all the pillar boxes had been repainted emerald green with an extra daub of paint to obliterate the cypher of what was now a foreign monarch.

For all the beauty of its surroundings no other port in the world has ever known such unending heartbreak. Few and blessed are the Irish families which remain intact when the children have reached the age of earning and through this pretty harbour and along this neat quay has ever flowed such a haemorrhage of native blood as no race should ever have to endure. For a few it is the gateway to opportunity but for the many it is the commencement of an exile which will last their whole life long.

The Royal Mail Steamer 'Munster' rocked gently at her mooring with as yet no more than a hundred passengers in her for her main complement were at that moment chugging along the twenty minute journey from Dublin's Westland Row station to begin what was for most of them the greatest adventure of their lives. Mostly they masked their apprehension with a cheerfulness not very far removed from tears although a few were grateful to be leaving a land with nothing to offer them but poverty and humiliation. For a few years they would return to show off their new clothes at Easter or to stand, strangers among their own kin, while their parents were placed in the ground and in time all they will have left of their homeland will be their name and a certain soft way of speaking. When their own race is run they will die in an alien place with few to mourn them. It is a sorry fate.

Rory Aylmer stood at the ship's rail capped and ulstered against the weather. Beside him a befurred Constance tucked her arm confidently through his as they watched the small activities on the quay below them.

'Though the last glimpse of Erin with sorrow I see' he sang softly and as she turned her face to him enquiringly he explained 'An old song. Called 'The Coolin' I think. They used to sing it in the village.' Then, because he had a need to be alone, he suggested 'Don't you think you had better be getting down to your cabin? We don't want you catching cold.' Nor did he want her to see in the Evening Mail folded in his hand that her kinsman Erskine Childers had been shot at dawn in Beggars Bush barracks for the crime of loving his adopted country too much. She would be bound to learn of it in London but it was best put off for as long as possible. He wondered what they would do with Childer's body, the body of Lieutenant Commander Erskine Childers the naval airman who had won the DSO in the war and who almost single-handedly had fathered the rebellion by his gun-running exploit when on leave in 1914. There would be no state funeral for Erskine Childers although he deserved one more than most. Much better he had stuck with his own people instead of squandering his life on people who did not know what gratitude was.

'It is cold' she agreed, pulling her fur collar about her slender throat. As she turned to go he asked her politely 'You're sure you can manage?' Of course she could manage. It was not her first time across the water. 'A26 I think it was.' He assured her it was A26, one of the best cabins in a ship where few people bothered taking private accommodation for the three hour crossing to Holyhead.

Alone at the taffrail he felt in his pocket for pipe and tobacco. When it was alight with the blue smoke rising like incense before his face he wondered again if they were doing the right thing even if there seemed to be no alternative. Like a persisting dream he saw again the hills around Gorteen and the nettle-lined road leading to the main gate of Ardnagoilte. Already he was missing Ardnagoilte although it was no more than a dozen miles away, say a good morning's tramp over country he knew so well that he could have done it with his eyes closed. The weeks spent in Dublin while matters were being arranged had not eased the pangs of parting from the old place and the old staff, for each and every one of them had been in the nature of family to him and he still worried about the Fogarty lad who might well have met the same fate as old Sheila and for the same ungood reason. The Admiral has been right. It was a terrible country. But a country to be loved just the same. No other land would ever take its place in his heart. Poor old Maggie Watkins had been quite distressed. All of them had been distressed but Maggie had taken it worst. Somehow he felt responsible for that also. Maybe if he had given it another year...

Down in the cabin Constance patted her still almost flat stomach. Reflected in the mirror her face seemed already to be glowing with the bloom of maternity. A sense of well-being flooded her body as if it was at last performing the only function for which it had been created and she knew with certainty that from now on nothing would ever trouble her again as all of life once had. Three weeks in London to look forward to. Maybe they would be married there. But if not, what matter? She already was Mrs Aylmer and, whether married to Rory or not, she would arrive in New Zealand as Mrs Aylmer, which was all that really mattered. She unhooked her dress and lay down on the bunk bed to be properly rested for Holyhead.

Up on deck Rory watched the straggle of passengers coming from the boat train, mainly youths on the threshold of manhood all in their best suits with tweed caps pulled down on their heads for it would have been presumptuous for any working man to wear a hat and almost all of them with the Sacred Heart pin of the Pioneer Temperance Association in the lapels of their jackets. Only a few wore overcoats. At first sight they looked just like people coming from Mass on Sunday except that people coming from Mass do not carry pathetic cases of cardboard or wicker secured by a piece of string and people

182

coming from Mass do not usually shriek with the hysterical laughter which strives to hide sadness or even fear. Big round faces, unalike in essence but with some undefinable factor in common, were turned to the ship, the first and certainly the largest vessel many of them had ever seen.

Now each and every one of them stood at the point of no return. Until they actually mounted the covered gangway they still had time to change their minds but once on board the die had been cast for good or ill. Until the boat train reached Euston they would be cushioned against the fact of exile by the company of their own kind, sharing a common heritage and relating to each other by virtue of their religion. For they would all be Catholics and the children of poor homes. No farmers' sons here. No sons of doctors, shopkeepers, civil servants or politicians. Untrained and inexperienced as the children they so recently were they began their battle for survival with only a few pounds in their pockets and rosaries blessed by their parish priest, with protective scapulars worn next the skin to ward off evil and perhaps to apprise some coroner that this was the body of an Irish Catholic.

Now they surged along the windswept quay, a solid mass of Irishry moving in invisible chains to the vessel which would carry them away from their native land as other vessels carried the cattle which were Ireland's next largest export.

'Misthur Rorey! Misthur Rorey!'

Rory looked down to the quay where someone was calling his name, some woman he had never seen in his life before and she in an advanced stage of pregnancy. Then he saw something of Larry Mangan in the bloated features and knew by that token that the person calling his name must be young Eileen who used to work in the kitchen of Ardnagoilte with Mrs Comiskey. But this could not be young Eileen. Eileen was still a child not yet eighteen and this woman who did bear a passing resemblance to her was at least ten years older. 'Are you Eileen?' he asked doubtfully. 'Eileen Mangan from Gorteen?'

'Av course I am' she called delightedly, her face turned upwards to him with that idiotic smile all the Mangans had. 'Shure wonders'll never cease as they say. Here I am on me wayta London without a soul to talk to an' who shows up before me very eyes but young Misthur Rorey hisself goin' the very same way so we can be company fer each other. An' hows tricks with you, Misthur Rorey? I heard tell maybe you'd be leavin' the big house an' its heartbroke ya must be for it's a lovely house so it is an' everything in the best've order.

The Englishman in him was acutely conscious that people nearby were listening with undisguised interest. 'What are you doing here?' he asked lamely.

He could not have asked a worse question. 'Me?' she shrieked at the top of her voice. 'Shure me mother thrun me out when she learneda the babby but Father Pethur took me to the nuns an' they fixed it up for me ta go ta what they call a hos-tel until the babby comes. Then they'll find me what they call suit-able employment. An' Father Pethur's goingta see Seamus knows where I am when he comes lookin' fer me. So that's all right. Maybe I can come an' work fer you in London.'

God forbid, he thought, wondering who this Seamus might be for it was not a name he remembered from Ardnagoilte and the girl seemed to think it would mean something to him. Wondering also what sort of woman would turn her own daughter out into the street but understanding there could be no place in Gorteen for an unmarried girl with a baby. And what kind of work would they find for her? Another big house probably. But young Eileen would find a great difference if it was for the English knew how to keep servants in their proper place. He wondered if he should try to give her some money, but already people were looking oddly at the well-dressed man talking to the obviously peasant girl and he did not dare risk it. Besides, he too hard to learn how to keep servants in their place but how he would do that he could not imagine.

'I am on my way to New Zealand' he told her unwisely. 'First London and then New Zealand in a few weeks time.'

'Is Herself with ya? Young Missus Aylmer I mane. All've us

thought you two'd hit it off wan day. Wouldya ever get her ta come an' say goodbye fer old times sake? Shure we were all fonda Miss Constance so we were.'

'She is resting' he told her shortly. In just a few moments shouted conversation all his business had been revealed to total strangers. 'Perhaps later' he temporised for the poor creature meant well enough and her trouble was far greater than any of his though she seemed not to be aware of that, smiling up at him with her big country face.

'Very well so' she shouted back, not one whit discomfited by the coldness of his tone. 'Well, maybe we'll meet on the train an' we can be together as far as London, can't we? Us Irish should always stick together.'

One thing which most certainly would never have entered his head was that he was the same Irish as the Mangans. Or Keogh. Or Nolan.

'Who dja think yer pushin'?' she snarled to a uniformed man who was trying to persuade her towards the after gangway and in one split second he saw her mother in her and thought that Seamus, whoever he might be, was well out of it although leaving a girl in that condition was hardly the done thing. Still it probably meant little to her. The way they lived they did not much bother where the children came from as long as there were plenty of them. Like rabbits, as the old Admiral said more than once. The bred like rabbits and with as little concern.

'Dont' ferget!' she screeched as the man turned her towards the steerage gangway. 'Look out fer me on the train. We can have a great oul' gas tagether.' Then she was gone to his great relief, still blackguarding the poor chap who had been sent to get the last remaining passengers on board.

The departure was subdued and too regular an occurrence to arouse any great interest in the town as the 'Munster' made ready to leave port in an orderly sort of bustle and a few gruff commands as if the cargo was not heartsick people fearful of what waited on the other side of the Irish sea.

Farewells had all been said at the doors of humble homes for the Irish are not great ones for seeing off by train or boat. And

185

they do their crying in private with many a whispered prayer to the Holy Mother of God to take care of Eilish or Seamus or Sean, to keep them safe from harm and to preserve them in the Faith. For full many a soul had been lost in the cities of sinful England. Many a grieving mother would not be able to sleep until the first ill-written letter arrived from over the water, and however many children might be their care the missing one would be a ghost at every meal, that voice heard first thing every morning and that footfall listened for as the shadows fell on their childhood home.

It is a devastating sorrow and blessed indeed are the Irish mothers who do not have to carry it like a piece of ice in the innermost recess of their hearts, wondering how the great God of heaven and earth could be so heedless of his most devoted creatures, how He who loved His own Blessed Mother could so disregard the prayers of other mothers here below. Then they would beg forgiveness for ever doubting His essential goodness. But the children would still be gone. And perhaps forever.

Huddled in rainstreaked jackets the longshoremen worked silently to cast off lines fore and aft and to drop the gangways back on the quay against tomorrow's sailing. As the vessel edged away from the land Rory took a few paces across the deck, as much an exile in the First Class midship section as were the embryo nurses and housemaids, the labourers and kitchen porters and the girls and boys who would become thieves and prostitutes under the stern lash of necessity within a matter of years though for now they concealed their fears in a sort of hysteria, calling to each other too loudly in the varying accents of their counties and townlands and laughing immoderately at unfunny jokes. For it was either that or crying aloud until no more tears were left in them.

The siren whauped and the ship shuddered as the screw slowly turned in a turbulence of its own making. The last link with the shore had been broken and already the lights of the town were falling away as if it and not the ship was in motion.

186

Watching the receding lights and unaware of the chilling wind Rory stood wooden-faced at the rail filled with a sick sense of misgiving. Never in his life had he ever thought he would end his days anywhere but Ireland. Now he was heading for a country of which he knew nothing other than what he had read in books. Inconsequential things troubled his mind. The priest. I should have done something about that priest. I should have called to thank him for taking my part that day but there had not been time. To be honest, there had been time but he had funked facing the villagers who had humiliated him and made him feel a stranger in the place he was born. Perhaps he would write when he reached London. Yes, that was it. A letter would be much more easy than what would have been a difficult conversation with half the village watching him go into the Presbytery and all of the village on hand to see him come out again. Mentally he started to compose the letter but go stuck with the very first words. 'Dear Father So-and-so' he would begin. But what on earth was the priest's name? Houlihan? Mulligan? Even if he only started it 'Dear Father' he would still need the name on the envelope for to address it simply to the Parish Priest of Gorteen would be insensitive and he ought to be able to remember it for he had heard it often enough. Milligan? That sounded more like it. But it would have to be correct for few things give more offence than forgetting a man's name.

It was no good. Like it or not he would have to see young Eileen again between here and Holyhead. At the same time he could slip her a few pounds for she would surely be in need of money and it would be what his mother would have wished. Gogarty? No, not Gogarty. He would have remembered that for they had been on dining terms with the Gogartys before all the trouble started. Nice chap Gogarty and a first-rate shot. Milligan seemed to have the right ring to it, but anyway Eileen would be able to tell him.

That light sweeping through gathering dusk would be Howth. For all that it was only on the other side of the Bay he had never been there. Now he would never have the chance. Except for the war he had never wished to go away from Gorteen unless for a business trip to Dublin which he did not particularly like. Now he was leaving as reluctantly as the meanest cottager or slum-dweller down below where they seemed to be having one of those hooleys they went in for at times of sorrow or rejoicing. From the steerage saloon down below he could hear an unknown man singing The Rising of the Moon in an alcoholic tenor to show the sea held no terror for him with a ragged chorus joining in the refrain with same rough laughter he had heard in France when fighting for England and Ireland had seemed to be the same uncomplicated thing. Now he felt a kinship with the unseen singer and knew that he was very close to tears. And that would never do at all.

As on a signal the singing ceased and there was the sound of scrambling feet as they all poured up the narrow companionway and flocked like birds at the ships rail, silent and with hearts too full for speech as they watched the shore of their homeland slipping away, perhaps forever. For all Irishmen have this in common: they all die a small death when they have to leave the land where their forefathers lie in mossed graves by crumbling cabins in places without a name. And go wherever they will on the face of the earth they will always hear the ancestral voices calling them back to a country which perhaps has not treated them well but which they will love while life is left in them. And however they may prosper in exile there will always be in them a languor of longing at the sound of an Irish voice or the mention of an Irish placename.

Now the moon had risen through a ragged gap in the clouds to shine a silvery track across the heaving surface of the bay. Hot tears burned behind Rory's eyes as he thought like a child If I could walk along that path of moonbeam and go by way of Killiney and Cabinteely to the Scalp, and then across the hill I could be at Ardnagoilte in time to see the sun rise on Knocknagowna and never leave it again for as long as I live.

And then a dog barked. Whether it was actually on the boat or only in his head he could not say, but he heard it clearly in his soul. And he knew that wherever he went in the world always he would hear a dog barking in the night and remember a small grave in a neglected rose garden and harden his heart against the country he was leaving as surely as scalding tears streamed down his tortured face at this moment. One bark only but he waited hoping to hear it again to be sure it really was old Sheila, perhaps telling him of a better land somewhere where men did not hate each other because of a shared god, where men might be judged by what they themselves did rather than by what their ancestors did. If such a place really existed then surely he would find the little priest from Gorteen waiting for him there.

The few other First Class passengers had retreated from the chill air and the stinging spray of the mounting seas. Huddled into his heavy overcoat he moved along the deck to the white painted rail which separated the classes, hearing the snarl of the wind in the halyards and ratlines and looking down on the small knots of people huddled together wherever they could away from the noise of the saloon where others were already being seasick in anticipation, for that too was part of the ordeal. Try as he would he could not decide if any of them was young Eileen Mangan and as he peered into the fitful light another snatch of song wafted upwards to him as a beer-drenched young voice sang

> 'I have no father to take my part
> I have no mother to break my heart
> But I have a friend and a girl is she
> Who would give her life for McCafferty.'

The words he had never heard before. But the tune he knew well because it was forbidden in the army, a tune which if even whistled in the hearing of an officer would have placed the whistler on a severe disciplinary charge. Quite why he did not know. Something to do with a mutiny somewhere. But why anyone should object to it he could not imagine for it sounded to be no more than another of those maudlin songs soldiers are given to.

A moment later he had his answer as a rough Dublin voice called 'Ah, yev got it all wrong, Jamesy. Thems not the words at all. These is the proper words' And then a deeper voice rose strongly to where Rory stood as if he was two persons or one person divided into two, one part identifying with the people below and the other part contemptuous of them and their slovenly ways which would make them to be forever a people unworthy of respect.

The words came to him clearly and in an assured voice and he could almost picture the singer as a stocky man tense as a coiled spring and with a flat Irish face, proud almost to arrogance and looking very much as Derry Keogh had looked marching his company through Gorteen as confidently as if he had been born to command.

The voice sang

> 'Twas early, early in the Spring
> The birds did whistle and sweetly sing
> Lifting their notes from tree to tree
> And the song they sang was 'Old Ireland Free.'

and verse after verse as a remembrance of the failed rebellion of the United Irishmen in 1798, born in the masonic lodges of the Presbyterian North and breathing its last on the bloodied slopes of Vinegar Hill in the county of Wexford when Catholic and Protestant fought and died side by side for the freedom and dignity of their common homeland.

As the last notes were torn away and scattered by the freshening breeze Rory thought that one thing would never change whoever ruled Ireland. The mournful songs of exile would still be sung as they were being sung now somewhere below where he stood gripping the rail with the wind lashing his cheek and the salt of the driving spray mingling with the salt of the unrestrained tears pouring down the taut mask of his face as the ship dipped into the swell and turned to bear him on the sad pilgrimage which is the destiny of the Irish.